"I heard you're looking for The Wolf."

Icy contempt flashed in agent Carson Turner's dark eyes. "Maybe."

"We need to talk."

"Outside. That is—" his gaze slid over her too-suggestive apparel with a frown "—if you can stand the cold. What makes The Wolf your business?"

"He's my brother." She cocked her head, considering. "He never mentioned you. Are you a friend?"

Instead of answering, he took a step closer. The back of her neck tingled, which meant the danger was great indeed.

"Do you know what your brother Alex is?"

"I do," she retorted, though she knew they were speaking of different things. "The question is, do you?"

Dear Reader,

Welcome to another month of excitingly romantic reading from Silhouette Intimate Moments. Ruth Langan starts things off with a bang in *Vendetta,* the third of her four DEVIL'S COVE titles. Blair Colby came back to town looking for a quiet summer. Instead he found danger, mystery—and love.

Fans of Sara Orwig's STALLION PASS miniseries will be glad to see it continued in *Bring On The Night,* part of STALLION PASS: TEXAS KNIGHTS, also a fixture in Silhouette Desire. Mix one tough agent, the ex-wife he's never forgotten and the son he never knew existed, and you have a recipe for high emotion. Whether you experienced our FAMILY SECRETS continuity or are new to it now, you won't want to miss our six FAMILY SECRETS: THE NEXT GENERATION titles, starting with Jenna Mills' *A Cry In The Dark.* Ana Leigh's *Face of Deception* is the first of her BISHOP'S HEROES stories, and your heart will beat faster with every step of Mike Bishop's mission to rescue Ann Hamilton and her adopted son from danger. Are you a fan of the paranormal? Don't miss *One Eye Open,* popular author Karen Whiddon's first book for the line, which features a shape-shifting heroine and a hero who's all man. Finally, go *To The Limit* with new author Virginia Kelly, who really knows how to write heart-pounding romantic adventure.

And come back next month, for more of the best and most exciting romance reading around, right here in Silhouette Intimate Moments.

Yours,

Leslie J. Wainger
Executive Editor

Please address questions and book requests to:
Silhouette Reader Service
U.S.: 3010 Walden Ave., P.O. Box 1325, Buffalo, NY 14269
Canadian: P.O. Box 609, Fort Erie, Ont. L2A 5X3

One Eye Open
KAREN WHIDDON

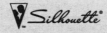

INTIMATE MOMENTS™

Published by Silhouette Books

America's Publisher of Contemporary Romance

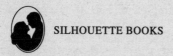 SILHOUETTE BOOKS

ISBN 0-373-27371-1

ONE EYE OPEN

KAREN WHIDDON

Karen Whiddon started weaving fanciful tales for her younger brothers at the age of eleven. Amidst the Catskill Mountains of New York, then the Rocky Mountains of Colorado, she fueled her imagination with the natural beauty of the rugged peaks and spun stories of love that captivated her family's attention.

Karen now lives in North Texas, where she shares her life with her very own hero of a husband and three doting dogs. Also an entrepreneur, she divides her time between the business she started and writing the contemporary romantic suspense and paranormal romances that readers enjoy, and that she now brings to Silhouette Intimate Moments. You can e-mail Karen at KWhiddon1@aol.com or write to her at P.O. Box 820807, Fort Worth, TX 76182. Fans of her writing can also check out her Web site at www.KarenWhiddon.com.

To my best friend and critique partner Anna Adams,
for all your valuable insight and immeasurable support—
thanks from the bottom of my heart.

And to Lucienne Diver, my agent.
Your unflagging belief and enthusiasm have
meant more than I can ever express. I appreciate you dearly.

Chapter 1

"I never pay for sex."

It took a minute for the tall man's words to register. When they did, Brenna suppressed a smile. "That's good, because I'm not selling it." She couldn't blame him for thinking she worked the seedy bar. Apart from two waitresses, she *was* the only female in the place. And the snug fit of her worn jeans with the black leather vest didn't help, either. Maybe that explained why she felt as if she was being watched.

"I want to talk to you."

The corners of his mouth twisted. "Sure you do."

She took a deep breath. "I heard you're looking for The Wolf."

Icy contempt flashed dark in his eyes. "Maybe."

"I have information," she lied. "I know him well."

From his skeptical expression, she could tell he didn't believe her.

"We need to talk." Though insistent, she kept her voice low, showing none of her rising impatience.

"Outside. That is—" his gaze slid over her, dismissing her too-suggestive apparel with a frown "—if you can stand the cold."

She'd worn the biker clothing to fit in. Gritting her teeth, she nodded once. Her heavy parka lay on the bar stool next to her. She picked it up and slid her arms into the sleeves without answering.

Outside, the full moon shone bright and silver through the threadbare tangle of trees that fringed the small parking lot. If she'd been a Hollywood-style werewolf, this man would be dead, his throat ripped out in seconds.

"Look, before we start—"

"I seldom pay for information, either," the man drawled. "And then only from known sources."

His words barely registered. There was something else… She sensed a threat in the frozen night breeze. Carefully she let her gaze drift past him to the dark and shadowy underbrush that surrounded them. Though she couldn't put her finger on it, there was wrongness to the night.

Someone was watching them.

Every nerve on edge, she forced her attention back to the stranger. "I don't want money. I want an even exchange. My info for yours."

His dark brows lifted. "What makes The Wolf your business?"

She would tell him her name, in case he knew of her. "I'm Brenna."

"So?" He made a dismissive motion with one gloved hand.

So he didn't know. Time, then, to play her trump card. "The Wolf is my brother."

Nothing on his rugged face indicated she'd shocked him. Instead, his insolent gaze again raked over her, making her shiver despite the warmth of her parka and relative anonymity of her hood.

"Sure he is."

Hounds help me, she thought, and clenched her jaw. "I'm telling the truth."

"Alex doesn't have a sister." His voice sounded flatly certain.

The use of her brother's first name jarred her. But only for a second. "You talk like you know him."

"I do—or did."

She cocked her head, considering. "He never mentioned you. Are you a friend?"

Instead of answering, he took a step closer. "Alex always said he had no family."

That stung. But only for a moment. Most likely Alex had tried to protect her.

Since she couldn't speak her thoughts out loud until she determined this man's intent, Brenna contented herself with a small smile and a shrug.

"Maybe you didn't know him as well as you thought."

He conceded her point with a dip of his head. "So you're a biker babe, huh? You don't look it now."

She dismissed the inconsequential remark with a shrug. "How I look doesn't matter. Your purpose for hunting my brother does. Why do you want him?"

His jaw tightened. "Personal reasons."

"Not an answer. Friend or foe?"

He laughed then, his breath a plume of white frost in front of his face. "Look, lady, it's ten below. I don't have the time or the inclination to stand here all night. Do you have information or not?''

Her sense of *wrongness* increased. The back of her neck tingled. Every sense urged her to change, which meant the danger was great indeed. She needed to stall this man until she could assess the risk, take care of it and then somehow get the information she needed.

But how? Ever since this stranger had appeared in the same places she'd haunted, asking questions about her brother, the same questions she herself had asked, she'd planned this confrontation. While normally her kind avoided conflict, retreating into the shadows, she'd known if she wanted to find Alex she had no choice but to deal with the threat, face-to-face.

''My information for yours.'' Lifting her chin, she tried to scent the night air unobtrusively. ''You go first.''

Harsh lines in his face belied his anger. ''I could run a check on you. One phone call and I'll know everything about you.''

She stared. ''Are you threatening me?'' Humans usually had sharper instincts.

''If you have reason to feel threatened.''

If he looked for arrest information on her, he would find nothing. She'd never broken a law in her life. Since blending in with humans was one of her people's first and most important rules, she, like most others of her kind, lived an exemplary life. She worked as the sole librarian in the tiny upstate New York town where she lived. A librarian on leave.

Having no fears of a police record, Brenna studied the human. His dark eyes carried many shadows; his rugged features bore an unmistakable stamp of pain.

She needed to find out what this man knew about her brother. Without causing him harm, if possible.

Though patience had never been her strongest virtue, she took a deep breath. "Please. I need to know. Why do you want to find Alex?"

He took a step closer, his long shadow menacing, though he kept his hands jammed in his coat pockets. "Do you know what your brother is?"

His words slipped like icicles down the back of her parka. "I do," she retorted, though she knew they were speaking of different things. "The question is, do you?"

A metallic click from the trees behind them made her spin. She'd once had the misfortune of being in the forest during deer hunting season, and she recognized the sound.

"Down!" she yelled, dropping to the pavement at the same time. To his credit the big man didn't hesitate, going to the ground immediately. A millisecond later the sharp crack of a gunshot confirmed her guess. With her preternatural hearing, she heard the bullet whiz past harmlessly.

Immediately another shot rang out, again barely missing them. She stayed down. Though she had many powers, immortality was not one of them. A bullet would do the same damage to her that it would to any human.

Her companion swore. "Stay here." Without waiting to see if she would obey his terse order, he was up and running for the trees, crouched low. Bemused, she watched him go, though her senses told her the shooter had fled.

Who had shot at them? Though this man's questions bothered her people, she doubted any of them would take such a drastic step. Especially since she was the only one who truly believed Alex's life was in danger. She alone was hunting for him; her goal was to find her brother and make certain he was safe. The sudden appearance of this stranger with his numerous questions worried her, confirmed her fears. Alex was in grave danger.

Again she inhaled. The icy sigh of the winter wind in the trees told her that the danger was past. Standing, she wiped the snow off the front of her wet jeans and waited for the stranger to return.

A moment later he did, jogging awkwardly in the soft snow. He slowed as he approached her. Narrow-eyed, he shot her a look more icy than the glaciers of her ancestral homeland.

"Who was it?" Moving with a speed that startled her, he grabbed her arm. "Are you with them?"

Anger flared, clogging her throat. Jerking away, she stepped backward. "With whom?"

"Right." He cocked his head. "I'm taking you into custody."

Custody. "So you are a cop?"

"Of sorts."

"Odd choice of words." Hands on hips, she stared at him, unafraid. "So you think you're arresting me? For what?"

"Your own protection, maybe?" His deep voice dripped with sarcasm.

"I had nothing to do with that gunshot."

"Maybe you did and maybe you didn't. Still, they've been trying to kill me for a long time. I wouldn't put it past them to send a woman. Either way, you're coming with me. As insurance."

About to protest again, Brenna reconsidered. Going

with this man might not be a bad thing, especially since she had no other leads to Alex's whereabouts. If she spent more time with this stranger, she might be able to get him to tell her what he knew. And if his intentions were evil, her physical presence might help keep her brother safe.

But she would make him suspicious if she seemed too eager.

"I don't even know your name," she said. "Or who you are or what exactly you do."

"Well, Brenna." The menacing way he spoke made her wonder. "You've had the bad luck of trying to prey on a DEA Agent. Special Agent Carson Turner. Pleased to meet ya."

Stunned more by his word choice—how he had known that she'd considered him prey—Brenna simply stared. After a moment she realized he was waiting for her to respond.

"D...E...A." She enunciated each letter deliberately. "Interesting."

"Come on." Indicating a snow-covered SUV, he reached again for her arm. "Let's go."

With a simple step she evaded him. "I want proof."

"Proof?" All but snarling the word, he reached into his pocket and, fumbling with his gloved fingers, withdrew a plastic covered ID, holding it up for her inspection.

"Drug Enforcement Agency," she read out loud. "Carson Turner, Justice Department."

"Yeah." Pocketing the ID, he flashed her a humorless smile. "That's me. Now get in the car."

She examined the black Tahoe parked to the side. It was one of only two four-wheel-drive vehicles amid the seven or eight motorcycles in the parking lot. He pressed his remote control, and the vehicle lights flashed as the doors unlocked.

"I need to get my bag from the car." She started forward.

"I'll get it," he said. "Toss me your keys."

Without another word she did as he asked. So he worked for a government agency—was that good or bad? Since Alex wouldn't do anything illegal, what would the DEA want with him? No one in the Pack used drugs of any kind. Doing so could seriously impair the ability to change, causing far greater damage than any brief moment of pleasure would be worth.

Climbing in after her, Carson tossed her duffel bag in the back seat and started the engine, turning on his wipers to clear the powdery snow from the windshield. She waited until he'd backed from the parking lot and pulled out onto the road before trying again.

"Tell me what you want with my brother."

He gave a rude snort, shooting her a look of fury that felt like a slap. "I thought you said you knew what your brother was."

Holding on to the shreds of her patience, she gave a slow shake of her head. "Alex disappeared over a year ago. No one in the Pack—" she stopped, heart in throat, then shook her head "—I mean, no one in my family has heard from him. I'm worried."

Only the quiet rumble of the motor broke the silence.

"You know, if I didn't need to keep my hands on the wheel, I'd clap," he said. "You sound really sincere. Family. Right. Academy Award material, that."

She gave him a blank look. "I don't understand."

"I'm not going to argue the point now, but I'll tell

you what—'' disdain underscored his savage tone. ''—when you level with me, I'll level with you.''

Having learned long ago that there was no way to deal with irrationality, she stared out the window at the dark landscape as it flashed past. Being called a liar was a new experience and one she couldn't say she particularly liked.

But none of that mattered. None of it mattered at all, if she could only find her brother and make certain he was safe.

''What, no elaborate explanations?'' Carson taunted. ''Surely Alex gave you a better cover story than that.''

''Enough.'' Turning to look at him, she was careful not to show her teeth. ''If you really believed I was a criminal, you would have searched me for weapons before allowing me in your truck. You'd need a hell of a lot more proof of some kind of crime before you could legally arrest me.''

He swore under his breath. She continued as if she hadn't heard him.

''So, in the spirit of honesty—and legality—'' she allowed a trace of her own anger to show in her voice ''—why don't you tell me why you're looking for my brother? Or I'll start to believe—'' she met his stare directly, ignoring the cynicism she saw there ''—that you yourself are engaged in some sort of illegal activity. I won't allow you to threaten my family.''

''Won't allow?''

Though she'd spoken one of the most important creeds of the Pack, he didn't seem to recognize it, which was good.

''No.''

He smiled. ''Short and sweet. I like that.''

Crossing her arms, she waited. Finally he shrugged. The look he gave her was laced with mistrust.

"Ever heard of Hades' Claws?"

Puzzled, she mentally reviewed every magazine article she'd read, every television show she'd watched, in preparation for this trip. "No."

His mouth thinned. "Right. The Wolf is your brother, but you don't even recognize the name of his biker gang?"

Biker gang? No way. Not Alex. Like her, he'd gone to college, gotten a good job. He worked in marketing, with a large Long Island firm.

"You must be mistaken," she said, her certainty showing in the flatness of her normally melodic voice. "Alex doesn't even own a motorcycle."

"Then why did you call him The Wolf? And why were you looking for him in a biker bar?"

She frowned. "The Wolf has been his nickname ever since third grade. And I heard he'd been to that bar, that's all."

With a quick motion, he peeled off his right glove, keeping his left hand on the wheel. Reaching into his coat pocket, he pulled out a much-folded sheet of paper and handed it to her.

Though grainy, the black-and-white photo in the center of the page was unmistakable. Alex.

Quickly she scanned the text. An FBI datasheet, the paper went on to describe how a biker gang, Hades' Claws, had committed numerous crimes, including several drug-related murders up and down the East Coast. Her brother was believed to be one of its high-ranking members and was wanted for questioning.

Feeling numb, she handed the paper back to Carson.

Accepting it, he kept his bleak stare on the darkened road ahead.

"Time to share again," he said. "Since you know why I'm looking for The Wolf, now you can tell me who shot at us."

She raised a brow. "Why do you think I would have that information?"

"You obviously were forewarned. You knew when to hit the ground."

"I heard the gun cock."

"Right," he said. "Who was the shooter?"

"I really don't know." She shrugged, careful to keep her expression neutral, while her head spun and her heart ached. Was the datasheet right? Was her brother hiding because he'd turned to crime? Or, as her premonitions suggested, was he in real danger?

"Damn." Carson went still, focusing on the rearview mirror.

Glancing over her shoulder, she saw headlights approaching fast on the otherwise deserted road.

"Are they—"

"Hold on." His low-voiced order was terse. He accelerated. The Tahoe leaped forward. The speedometer crept past eighty, then eighty-five. Ninety. The cab began to vibrate. She hoped that the road would remain straight and flat; at this speed, the slightest curve might send them into a skidding rollover.

Checking to make sure her seat belt was securely fastened, Brenna glanced over her shoulder. If they were going over ninety, the other vehicle had to be traveling in excess of one hundred, for it still seemed to be steadily gaining on them.

''I can't kill the headlights.'' Carson swore again.

A green highway sign loomed ahead. Wicket Hollow—One Mile.

''I'm gonna take it,'' he said. Still, he kept his foot on the accelerator, his hands locked in place on the steering wheel.

''Not at this speed. If we crash—''

''We won't.''

Oddly enough, his calm certainty appeased her. She bit the inside of her cheek, forcing herself to relax her death grip on the door handle.

She told herself not to be afraid. Yet one thing kept running through her mind. If they crashed and she was mortally injured, she would be unable to keep from changing. She would have to drag herself away from the crash scene and die in her natural state far from human eyes. This was the law of her people. To do otherwise would risk bringing discovery and possible ruin upon them all.

Closing her eyes, Brenna began to plan. Just in case.

''There's the exit.''

At his words, she opened her eyes. ''Too fast,'' she snapped, as they blasted past the sign and left the highway.

''Seventy-five.'' Satisfaction sounded in Carson's voice. ''One curve, then, straight shot.''

She sat up. They were on the access road. Trees blocked the highway from view.

''Are they gone?''

''Not yet.'' Violence still sounded in his voice. ''There.'' Pointing to a dirt road that wound into the trees, he killed the headlights and slowed. Pulling into a thicket, he parked.

Then they waited, the sound of their mingled breathing harsh and loud in the quiet interior.

A moment later a vehicle sped past, too quickly in the darkness for Brenna to make out its type.

"Hummer," Carson said, as if he'd read her mind. "Dark colored—black, brown or blue. Whoever they are, they've got money."

Swallowing, she nodded. Still her heart pounded in her chest. She willed it to slow.

"We need to go," she said.

"In a minute." Leaning against his door, Carson spread his arm comfortably along the back of the seat. "Why don't you start talking? Are these the same people who shot at us?"

"I don't know."

"Enough lies." His tone lined with steel, he sat up and dropped his arm.

When she only stared silently at him, he swore again, his mouth twisting. With a savage flick of his wrist, he started the ignition. Once out of their hiding place, he pulled back onto the highway, continuing north.

Brenna watched the speedometer climb to eighty again, unable to resist a quick glance behind them at the now-deserted highway.

"No headlights." Carson confirmed. "Tell me the truth. Are you working with them?"

"Working with—" She shook her head. "Of course not. I don't believe in random violence."

He regarded her strangely. "Your brother does."

"My brother's in trouble," she muttered. "I don't know how or why, but he is."

His short bark of laughter contained no humor. "In trouble? Of course he is. Besides having the DEA,

ATF and FBI after him, he has to worry about rival gangs. It's only a matter of time until one of us finds him. I wouldn't want to be in your brother's shoes right now.''

There was something in his voice. Pain. Bitterness. Rage.

''It's more than that with you,'' she said, keeping her eyes on his shadowed profile.

At that his head snapped up, his gaze icy again. ''What do you mean?''

''You're too angry. With you, it's personal.''

She thought he might deny it, even as the fury that momentarily darkened his eyes betrayed him. But after a moment of chilly silence, he gave her a cold smile and nodded.

''My wife and daughter are dead because of Hades' Claws.'' He might have been discussing the weather, so remote was his voice. ''They thought they'd killed me, too.''

His unspoken anguish sliced through her, sharper than any knife. ''Were you shot?''

''In the back. I nearly died. Now I want the ones who killed my family.''

She swallowed. ''Surely you don't think Alex was part of that.''

''Yeah, actually, I do.''

She couldn't believe it. There were a hundred reasons why Alex couldn't be the killer he sought, but she couldn't give him any of them.

''Now.'' With one hand on the steering wheel, he grasped her chin with the other. ''I want the truth. Are those goons who shot at us and chased us Hades' Claws?''

Furious, **Brenna** tried to pull away, but he wouldn't

let her. "How would I know? If Alex is, as you say, involved with this gang, he wouldn't let them endanger me."

His expression turned dark. "They want me dead. They should have killed me when they had the chance. Now they'll have to wait until I'm done."

"Wait until—" She stared at him. "Are you saying you want to die?"

"Not until I find the people who destroyed my life."

He hadn't said no. What kind of man...? But she knew. He hurt. Like a wounded animal, Carson would seek death rather than continue to endure horrific pain.

Shaken, she looked away. There was no way she could fathom such grief.

"If you're in on this, now's your chance to come clean. I can get you government protection if you testify."

"I'm not in on anything. Alex would never..." She didn't bother to finish.

"I'll shut up about it for now," Carson finally said. "But if you're not with them, you're in danger. Hades' Claws mean business."

This time she smiled. "I can take care of myself."

"Sure you can." His mocking tone belied his words. "If you really are Alex's sister, you'd be real good at looking out for number one."

Every time he spoke her brother's name, she could taste the hostility.

"I *am* his sister," she said. "And if you knew him at all, you would understand why I can't believe my brother killed your family." The words stuck to her tongue. She tried again. "I don't understand how you can think he did."

He spoke a vile word under his breath. In the dim light, his features appeared savage, so like one of her people at the moment of change that she stared.

"Understand this, then. I was there. I was shot, but I saw Alex. He had a gun."

Chapter 2

Stunned, Brenna swallowed. "Alex couldn't," she stammered, her words trailing off at the cynical certainty she read on his face.

"The killing was a test to determine Alex's loyalty. They said he passed with flying colors."

A sound escaped her, something between a plea and a moan. She had read about this case. "The newspapers said an unnamed biker."

"Innocent until proven guilty. How could you not know? You're his sister." He made the simple sentence sound like a curse. "Or so you claim."

He thought her brother was a murderer. Worse, he believed she knew and was lying through her teeth. Her throat felt tight, closed in. She couldn't seem to get enough air. She forced herself to breathe deeply. To swallow then lift her head and look directly at Carson Turner, unflinching. Alex couldn't have done what this man claimed.

"There has to be some other explanation," she said. "You were shot. In pain. Maybe you saw wrong. Alex isn't a murderer."

Though in effect she'd just called him a liar, to his credit he didn't threaten or sneer. He didn't open the door and shove her out with a wave and a quick *hasta la vista,* baby. No, Carson did none of those things. He merely continued to regard her much like a wolf watches a rabbit caught in a snare, waiting for her to prove her statement.

But she couldn't, not in words he would believe. She hadn't been there; she hadn't seen her brother with a smoking gun. Carson had. Or thought he had.

"What kind of trouble are you in?" Carson asked, breaking into her chaotic thoughts.

Still silent, she shook her head, raising her hands, palms up, in a gesture meant to convey ignorance.

His mouth twisted. "If you want me to help you, you're gonna have to tell me."

Startled, she met his gaze. "Help me? Why would you do that?"

"Because whoever you are, I'm stuck with you right now." His sour tone left no doubt as to his feelings about the situation. "If you really are Alex's sister, having you with me might help me get his attention. If you're not," he shrugged, "you still seem to care deeply for him. Either way, your being with me can't hurt."

His eyes narrowed. "If you know something about the shooting or those guys in the Hummer, you'd better tell me now. Traveling with me is dangerous. You're putting your own life in danger."

"No," she told him. "I don't know anything." In more ways than one, she thought. Whatever Alex had gotten himself involved in, *dangerous* didn't seem to begin to describe the situation.

"Okay. I consider you warned." He sounded oddly agreeable—pleasant, even—making her wonder if he used this tone on a daily basis to trick suspects under interrogation into admitting guilt.

"You really think I'm a criminal." She spoke her thoughts out loud.

"The men in the Hummer weren't with law enforcement." He spoke as though he had no doubt. "Neither was the shooter."

She shook her head. "Hades' Claws?"

He snorted. "You tell me."

"Hey, I don't even know them." She could tell from Carson's skeptical expression that he didn't believe her. "Seriously, I never heard of Hades' Claws until you mentioned them."

"How long have you been looking for your brother?"

She narrowed her eyes. "A few months. I haven't heard from him for six. Why?"

"Surely you read the papers."

"Some." She gave a halfhearted shrug. "But I don't remember seeing anything about them."

He laughed then, lightening the grim atmosphere in the Tahoe. "Are you from around here?"

"No. Upstate. I came down here looking for my brother. Why?"

"Because they make the paper here all the time. Maybe your local paper isn't interested."

"So they aren't that bad?" Keeping her expression haughty, she resisted the urge to chew on her fingernail. This was a habit she'd broken in her teens, right after she'd passed the Pack tests that made her a full-fledged huntress. Odd that a habit she despised would try to resurface now.

"Oh, they're bad, all right. Unless you don't count murder, smuggling—" he ticked the words off on his fingers "—illegal weapons, drugs and robbery as wrong."

"And they want to kill you," she said softly.

"Oh yeah. And even if you can't get a grip on the idea that your brother is one of them, while you're with me you're a target, too."

"I'm not worried." She ran her fingers through the back of her long hair, combing it out from force of habit. "As I've said, I can take care of myself."

"So you claim." He lifted one shoulder in a quick shrug. "Either way, I have no intention of letting you out of my sight. So don't even think about taking off."

"The thought never crossed my mind," she drawled.

Instead of replying, he accelerated. At her questioning look, he flipped his fingers at the dark road ahead of them. "We need to get off the interstate."

"Do you think they'll catch us?"

One corner of his mouth twisted. "Eventually. For a while they'll keep going down that access road, thinking we're just ahead of them. But once they realize we pulled off somewhere…" As he spoke, he glanced in the rearview mirror.

His profile seemed hard and angry. No doubt he still believed she'd lied about her connection to the biker gang.

Biker gang. Alex a murderer. Hard to even think of using the words together in a sentence. Never mind DEA and FBI. Another shiver went down her spine.

"I'm not a member of Hades' Claws." Her words came out in a furious, staccato burst.

"A rival gang?"

"Of course not. No."

"You don't sound too certain. What about this 'pack' you mentioned?"

Alarm clogged her throat. He'd caught her accidental slip. "It's a nickname, an inside joke among my relatives," she said. "It's what we call ourselves. No gang, just family. You know how family can be."

"Yeah. I had a family once." The grim savagery in his voice made her catch her breath.

"How long ago?" she asked softly. "How long ago did it happen?"

He shook his head, a muscle working in his jaw. With a white-knuckle grip, he held on to the steering wheel. "It's been eighteen months."

Eighteen months. Last year, early spring. Alex had called her, told her he'd taken a new job, one that would let him move from the city back to the Catskills. Still only a few hours away, he'd said, knowing she missed him. After they'd graduated from college, he'd left her once before to go alone on an extended winter tour of the northern cities. Seattle, Vancouver, Boise, Helena, Bismark. Then east to check out Phillie and Boston and New York. His absence had made her sad, then furious, wishing she'd gone with him.

When he'd finally returned to the small town of Leaning Forest, he'd told wonderful stories. Not of blood or murder or mayhem, but of ordinary, city-human things. Rush hour and crowded subways, poodles with painted toenails and corner hot-pretzel vendors.

They'd laughed together over his tales. In her quiet

life as the town librarian, she'd secretly envied him the adventure, the experience, never dreaming that one day she would venture forth from her comfortable existence in search of him. Never expecting him to go missing, be accused of murder. How peaceful her old life seemed now.

"Eighteen months," she repeated. "And you've looked for revenge ever since?"

"I've been looking for your brother," he said. "As soon as I got out of the hospital, I started searching. Alex went underground. Obviously, he doesn't want me to find him."

She let that one go, focusing on the word *hospital*. He'd said he'd nearly been killed. "Did it take you a long time to recover?"

He gave a curt nod.

Less than two years. In her own life, a lot had happened in that time. She'd lost a fiancé, misplaced her brother. Meanwhile, this man's entire family had been ripped away, brutally murdered in circumstances that made her brother look guilty.

"I'm sorry." She knew her words were inadequate, but she meant them nonetheless.

In response, Carson accelerated again.

Brenna got the message and closed her mouth. The digital clock on the dashboard showed 1:30 a.m. Late for humans, but prime hunting time for those of her kind. Glancing at the shadowy woods as they flashed past, she wondered if any of her people roamed there. Snow had begun to fall, the dainty white flakes becoming thick, heavy ones the farther north they traveled. Soon Carson slowed the vehicle to a crawl, his headlights reaching only a few feet ahead of them on the snow-covered road.

A sign proclaimed they were on the outskirts of Albany, the state capital.

"Where are we going?" she asked.

"I got a lead that some of the gang is holed up in Hawk's Falls, near the Vermont border."

Mostly wilderness. Her kind of place. She allowed herself a small smile. As a huntress, her tracking skills were unparalleled. If Alex hid anywhere in a forest, she would find him.

"How long before we get there?"

He shook his head in the clumsy manner of a wolf cub shaking off snow. "We won't get there tonight," he said, his deep voice sounding gravelly. "It's late, and the storm's getting worse. I need some sleep."

She sat up. "I'm not tired. I'll drive."

He drummed on the steering wheel. "I don't think so."

"I want to find him as much as you do," she reminded him. "You sleep, I'll get us there. It's not too far."

"We're pulling off at the next town. We'll take a motel room for the night."

"But—"

"We have to stop sometime."

"I'll stop when I find my brother."

He shook his head again. "We'll start fresh in the morning."

"If we're not snowed in."

"I've got chains." He shrugged. "And there's always a plow."

She tried not to grind her teeth. "Look, I really think—"

"Enough." His tone was sharp enough to cut a coyote off in mid-howl. "This is not a democracy.

We're stopping and getting some rest. End of subject."

Brenna glared. "Fine. You get a room. I'll stay in your vehicle."

"Right." He snorted. "It's ten below and snowing, and you want to stay here?"

Put that way, her words did sound… unusual.

"I don't want to waste money on a motel room. I can rest here. This is comfortable enough for me."

"Money?" He gave her a long look. "Don't worry about it. I'll pay. We're sharing a room, anyway."

At her sputter of protest, he flashed her a bleak, tight-lipped smile. "Look, I'm not going to attack you. I don't want sex with the sister of my family's killer. I'll make sure we have two beds."

Safe. If only he knew. She suppressed the desire to growl. "I'm not worried."

"Of course not." His tone mocked her. "But like I said, until we find Alex, I'm not letting you out of my sight."

"I don't want to be that close to you."

"Tough."

She took a closer look at the intense man beside her.

"Fine," she conceded. "I want to keep an eye on you as badly as you do me."

"Then it's settled." In silence he drove on, windshield wipers slapping ineffectively against the blinding snow. He handled the vehicle with the ease of long familiarity. In the blizzard, the streetlights shone like dim halos, the occasional car or semi looming up huge, then lumbering away, like brief scenes from a surreal, homemade movie.

An exit sign indicated available lodging. They left

the freeway, turning right and fishtailing on the snowy road.

"Slow down," she said.

Instead of commenting, he pointed. "There." Clustered together were several older motels. A red neon sign at the first one indicated a vacancy.

Carson pulled into the snow-covered lot, parking around back, out of sight of the brightly lit office. With the snow coming down fast and furious, the place looked cozy, inviting, though Brenna knew in harsh sunlight the weather-beaten exterior would seem tired and worn.

With an innate caution that came as naturally as breathing, she took stock of her surroundings. The frame building appeared badly maintained, its fading green paint peeling. A few pine trees, bent and sickly, grew near the office. The weight of the snow on their branches made them seem about to topple.

Despite the storm, or perhaps because of it, the parking lot contained five or six other vehicles, all older, all rapidly disappearing under white shrouds of snow. From the iron bars on the office windows, she judged this would not be a safe place for a woman to wander at night, at least a human woman unable to change.

Carson killed the ignition and pocketed the key before turning to face her, his expression flat.

"Let's go." He squeezed her shoulder, effectively cutting off her last attempt at refusal. "Give it up. You're staying with me."

"I'm your captive?" Both amused and angry, she couldn't help but wonder at his reaction if she were to change right here, right now. If she were her powerful wolf self, he wouldn't be able to contain her.

No man on earth could hold her then. Even as a human, she was a formidable opponent. Years of martial arts classes had made sure of that.

For now she could only let him think he had won. The force of his glare told her he didn't appreciate her amusement or her anger.

"Fine," she said. "Let's go."

"Brenna, I'm warning you." Illuminated by the flashing neon hotel light, his gaze was as cold as the night and twice as harsh. "Don't try to escape. Your brother destroyed my family and ruined my life. I *will* make him pay. Neither you nor anyone else will be able to stop me."

Releasing her, he pushed open his door and strode around to her side. Before he reached the door handle, she pushed it open herself and slid to the ground in front of him. Squaring her shoulders in the bulky parka, she lifted her chin and stared him in the face, snow swirling around both of them in a heavy cloud.

"My brother is not the man you're looking for."

"Unwavering devotion," he drawled. "That's good in a sister." Pausing, he looked her over once. "That is, if you really are Alex's sister."

Her breath came out in a hiss. Narrow-eyed, she glared at him with such ferocity that he took a step back. Then she spun on her heel and marched over to the hotel office, yanking open the dirty glass door. She went inside without waiting to see if he would follow.

A few minutes later, metal key firmly in hand, Carson allowed her to precede him toward their room.

On the ground floor, 119 sat at the very back of the building, as far away from the growl and snarl of the normal freeway traffic as the hotel offered.

Though the blizzard muffled sound, she was still glad, as the noise, utterly foreign, made her uncomfortable and restless.

Come to think of it, the utter absence of sound, normally welcome, had her feeling skittish as well. Or maybe she owed her heightened awareness to her companion. With his grim-jawed features, he appeared oblivious to her discomfort as he unlocked the door.

Once inside, he flicked the light switch. A single dim lamp illuminated the well-used room.

Brenna went in. She sniffed, wrinkling her nose at the foul smell. Though he'd asked for nonsmoking, the stale scent of cigarettes hung in the musty air. Coughing, she looked at the window. Carson shook his head.

"Too cold." A battered heat/air unit, faded yellow, sat under the window. With the twist of a knob, he turned on the heat. She could only hope the warmth didn't intensify the nauseating smell.

"I've been in worse," he said. Never having stayed in a motel, Brenna didn't reply. She waited to see what he would do next.

Two double beds took up nearly all the space in the room. Once he'd pulled the door closed behind him and turned the dead bolt, he had to turn sideways to get past her. Their chests brushed. He jerked away as though she'd given him an electrical shock. She couldn't help it—a quick chuckle escaped her at his discomfort.

Ignoring her, he moved quickly, turning on every lamp. The cheap clock radio on the nightstand blinked red—2:05 a.m. Then Carson went to the bed nearest

the door and yanked back the sour-smelling bedspread.

"Nice and comfy, don't you think?" His tone
mocked both her and their surroundings. The heat
overpowered her. The sickening odor made her head
spin. Because she didn't trust herself to speak without
giving her true nature away, she went into the tiny
bathroom and closed the door with a sharp click.

Chipped turquoise tile decorated the walls and
floor. The porcelain sink, though old, appeared clean.
She turned the faucet. The tap water felt icy and re-
freshing. Splashing her face, she drank deeply from
her cupped hands. Then she finger-combed her hair,
eyeing herself in the distorted mirror. Exhaustion and
worry had made faint circles under her brown eyes
and carved new hollows in her narrow face. She
craved a long hot shower, but she didn't want to leave
Carson alone for too long. If he made a phone call,
she wanted to hear every word.

By the time she came out of the bathroom, he had
pushed one of the beds snugly up against the front
door, effectively blocking them in.

"Yours?"

He nodded.

"Give me a break. What if there's a fire?"

"Then we'll move it."

Unable to resist pointing it out, she said, "There's
always the window."

"You'd have to go over me to get to it."

Over him. The air felt suddenly charged. Brenna
shrugged away the unfamiliar feeling of awareness
with a quick toss of her head.

"We can keep this up all night," he said. "Or we
can get some rest. It's late." Massaging the back of

his neck, he indicated the other bed. "That's yours. Go to sleep. We'll start again early in the morning."

"If the plows show up."

He gave her a tired smile. "They will. They always do."

He watched while she gingerly tested her mattress. She pinched a corner of the faded bedspread between her index finger and thumb, yanking it back so it fell on the floor at the foot of the bed. The nappy blanket, though, she turned back neatly. Then, still fully dressed, she lay down on her side on top of the sheets, trying to ignore the faint musty scent that tickled her nose. Still facing him, she kept her eyes open. Watching.

"Tap on the wall," he said.

Blinking, she sat up. "What?"

"I need to go in there." He indicated the bathroom. "I want you to tap on the wall until I come out."

Amused, she let her mouth curve in the beginnings of a smile. "You really think I'll run."

"Won't you?"

Exhaling loudly, Brenna lifted one shoulder. "Turn down the heat." Moving with deliberate slowness, she peeled off her heavy leather vest and tossed it on the bed. Then she lifted her hand to the wall and rapped three times, the plaster rough against her knuckles, repeating until she'd found a simple, primitive rhythm. Oddly, this soothed her.

After flipping the dial to off, he nodded curtly. Leaving the door slightly ajar, he spent less than a minute in the tiny bathroom before he emerged. Without glancing at her, he went around the room, extinguishing the lights one at a time. That made Brenna want to laugh again. She saw as well in the darkness as she did in the light.

She let her arm fall, watching him as he readied for bed.

Like her, he didn't undress. She heard the rasping sound of his jeans as he slid between the sheets, fully clothed.

In the silence, she listened for his breathing to slow. Instead his restless movements indicated he was as far away from sleep as she.

"Let me tell you about my brother," she said finally, keeping her voice low and nonconfrontational.

He grunted. "Go to sleep."

"Maybe I can tell you something you don't know."

"I doubt it."

"Alex and I are twins."

He sat up at her words, his bulky shape ominous in the dim light. "Listen, quit the lies. You're not even his sister. Alex had no family. Believe me, I would know if he did."

She sighed, reaching over and clicking on the light. "Maybe you don't know him as well as you think."

"You don't even look like him." Disgust colored his words, and his hard tone would have shaken even a career criminal. "He's blond and you're dark."

"We're fraternal twins."

"Sure." He folded his arms across his chest. "You live in fantasy land, lady."

She sighed again. "This is getting old. I'm telling the truth. Alex is my twin. I have no reason to lie."

"Don't you now?"

Ignoring his skepticism, she continued doggedly. "Alex and I are different in a lot of ways. Of the two of us, he is calmer and more rational."

"Alex is an unemotional man," he agreed, the savagery in his voice surprising her. "And I still don't believe you're his sister."

She leaned forward to peer at him through the dim light. "Did you ever see his birthmark? The one on his arm?"

Surprise briefly lit his face. "Yeah, I did," he said grudgingly. "I thought it was a tattoo at first."

Turning her back to him, she lifted her shirt, pushing down the waistband of her jeans so he could see. "The shape of a wolf," she said, giving him a clear view of her own birthmark above her left hip. "Maybe you'll believe me now."

He swore at the unmistakable evidence. "He never mentioned family. Any family. At all."

Ignoring that she let her shirt fall back into place, turning once more to face him. "You never told me. Where do you know Alex from?"

"DEA." He spat the single word. "We were undercover together. Alex was my partner."

Chapter 3

"Partner?" For a moment she didn't understand. Then, once she realized what he meant, she wanted to call *him* the liar. "You're telling me that my brother was working for the FBI?"

"DEA."

"Whatever." She swallowed. "He would have told me."

With a wry twist of his mouth, Carson shook his head. "He couldn't. Right after we graduated from Quantico, we were sent out together. We were both undercover."

Her heart skipped a beat. "Isn't that dangerous?"

"Very." From the hitch in his voice, she knew he was thinking of his murdered family.

"No wonder he didn't mention me," she said. "He didn't want to put me in danger."

With a pointed glance at the clock, which now showed 2:45 a.m., Carson made a rude sound. "Who knows? Who cares? Turn off the light and go to sleep.''

Stung, she glanced away. No matter what precautions her brother had taken, she'd managed to put herself at risk by traveling with Carson. Judging from the shooter and the men in the Hummer, danger had found her.

Reluctantly she clicked off the light and closed her eyes.

Morning came quietly, with bright sunlight peeking through the heavy curtains. The second she opened her eyes, Brenna lay motionless, instantly alert, and listened for activity outdoors.

''The snow's stopped.'' Carson spoke from near the door. How had he known she was awake?

Slowly she raised her head. Even with his five-o'clock shadow and sleep-mussed hair, the man looked devastatingly attractive. Dangerous. She licked her lips. ''I haven't heard the snowplows.''

''They haven't made it through yet.'' He ran a hand through his disheveled hair. ''I think we got maybe a foot.''

Forcing herself to look away, she swung her legs over the side of the bed. ''Powder?''

''I can't tell. Probably, under the crust. We'll find out. There's a coffee shop across from the motel office.''

She stretched, yawning. Though her jeans were snug, they were comfortable and she'd slept well in them.

''I'd like to take a shower.'' She rubbed the palms of her hands on the faded front of her jeans. ''That way I'd feel more human.'' Now there was a laugh.

Carson opened his mouth to reply, but whatever he'd been about to say was drowned out by a burst of static as the clock radio alarm on her nightstand went off.

The previous occupant must have set it. Shocked, she saw it read 10:00 a.m. They'd slept late.

"Breaking news." The radio announcer's stern voice broke into the dying strains of the music.

"Drugs were involved in a multiple murder in the small town of Welkory near the Vermont border."

They looked at each other. Swallowing, Brenna grimaced and reached to turn up the volume.

Details followed. In the midst of a bank robbery less than an hour earlier, two groups of people had opened fire on each other, killing several innocent bystanders. One of the getaway cars had been captured, trunk loaded with cocaine. Supposition was that the robbery had been an attempt to gain money to pay for the drugs.

"Damn," Carson said as the news announcer switched to another story. "That's north of Hawk's Falls. We need to check it out."

"The Claws?"

"Hades' Claws," he corrected absently. "And yes, I'm willing to bet they had something to do with it, especially since Welkory is so close to their hideout. Add the cocaine, and it's pretty much a given."

Again she met his gaze, letting him see her fierce determination. "You think Alex was involved, don't you?"

He shrugged, turning away. "No doubt."

Brenna took a long look at the man who'd claimed her as his captive. In the small room the pain radiated from him so strongly it made her own heart ache with sympathy she could ill afford. She needed to focus only on finding her brother and ensuring his safety.

"Let's go," Carson said.

"Wait." She held up a hand. "We need to get something straight. Your family is gone. You want revenge. I've got that. But I want to know the truth. You said you knew Alex well, that he was your partner. Well, why would he go bad? Is it possible there was some other explanation why he was at your house when it happened? Some other reason he had a gun?"

The absolute silence in which he glared at her was the embodiment of rage. Though the muscle that ticked in his clenched jaw should have been adequate warning, she couldn't stop herself from continuing.

"What do you think he did? Really? Murder, rape, torture?" The mere notion of someone thinking her twin could hurt anyone for no reason, anyone at all, made her furious. "He's incapable of those things. You should know that, too—if you truly know him as well as you say."

Despite her taunts, Carson said nothing. His features seemed cast in stone. Implacable. Angry. Hurt. She noticed he, too, wore the same faded jeans and dark flannel shirt as the night before. And boots. The man wore cowboy boots made of some kind of exotic leather.

"Somehow I have to prove to you that my brother is not the devil incarnate."

"You only have to prove it to yourself." Bitterness coated his words with acid. "Grab your coat. We're hitting the road. Since the robbery was less than an hour ago, the investigation will be in full swing." He consulted his watch. "The interstate should be plowed. If we leave now, we'll get there in time to talk to them.''

For the space of a heartbeat, she merely looked at him. ''Logic,'' she drawled. ''The one thing I can't argue with.''

A few minutes later they were back on the road. He'd been right about the snowplows. Piles of snow lined the one open lane on each side. Carson constantly pressed the Seek button on the radio, looking for more news about the robbery.

The farther north they went, the less deeply the snow appeared to blanket the ground. The highway opened up, too, all lanes, though the traffic seemed considerably lighter than the day before.

Welkory, Exit One Mile.

As they approached the turnoff, he reached behind him and yanked a wrinkled black jacket from behind the seat.

''Here,'' he said, shoving it into her lap. ''Put this on over yours.''

Noting the yellow DEA on the back, she guessed the coat would provide cover as well as warmth. Shrugging out of her own parka, she slipped on the lighter jacket. ''What about you?''

''I've got a cap.'' His tone discouraged conversation.

The two-lane road that led to Welkory was curved and lined with towering, leafless trees. Coated with a light dusting of snow, they appeared both majestic and threatening. Brenna sensed the presence of animals in the woods, though she and Carson sped by so fast that she had no time to communicate with any of them. Before long they rounded the final curve and found themselves smack-dab in the middle of Welkory.

Downtown seemed oddly deserted, as though at the first hint of danger all the shops had rolled up their carpets and locked their doors.

Carson slowed the car, though every one of the four stoplights turned green at his approach. First Street, flanked by well-maintained, charming historical buildings. Then Second and Third, until finally they reached the intersection of Main Street and Fourth. Yellow police tape squared off the corner of Welkory First Bank and Trust, and a yellow fire truck, lights flashing, was parked next to the drive.

Brenna counted no fewer than seven police cruisers, two of them local, the rest state police.

Carson rolled down his window to flash his ID at the officer blocking the entrance. "DEA," he barked and was rewarded with an immediate wave past the barricade. They barely glanced at Brenna. Wearing Carson's jacket made her look like another DEA agent.

He parked between two police cars, right next to the building. After turning off the ignition, he pocketed the keys and grabbed a battered black cap and crammed it on his head. The DEA letters in yellow made the cap a mate to her jacket.

"Ready?" he asked, his voice raspy. All traces of emotion had vanished from his face. He looked every part the professional government officer, stern and unforgiving in his quest for justice.

She licked lips suddenly gone dry before she replied quietly, "Yes."

"Then let's go," he said. "More than anyone else, you need to see this."

She heard the unspoken second part of his sentence: so you'll understand what kind of man your brother has become.

Eager to prove him wrong, Brenna pushed open her door. Ice-coated gravel crunched underfoot as she walked beside Carson to the squat brick building. Crisp air carried a chill that had nothing to do with the temperature and everything to do with the grim mood radiating from the uniformed officers who congregated inside the bank.

Brenna froze, sensation overwhelming her. The interior of this place smelled strongly of fear, of blood and death, like a hunt gone brutally wrong. She wanted to cover her nose, so nauseated did the scent make her. The odor of evil hung in the air so strongly she thought she might be sick. More than anything, she wanted to break away, lunge for the door and run. But she was a huntress, strong not weak. Though her sense of smell was ten times more powerful than a human's, she would force herself to stay.

She breathed, though each lung full of air felt cloying, full of decay and hate. She swallowed, tasted bile and concentrated on not being weak. Nothing, not the hunting rituals of the Pack, nor any of the limited television shows she watched, had ever prepared her for the carnage here.

Mindless savagery. Hate. Pure evil.

It felt surreal and simultaneously more real than any experience had ever felt. She despised every minute, wishing she were somewhere, anywhere, else.

Three sheet-covered bodies lay in front of the long, paneled counter. One man, probably the coroner, knelt beside the nearest one, making notes. Quiet sobbing came from a group of people clustered in the back.

"Tellers and other customers, most likely," Carson told her, *sotto voce*. "The ones who survived to tell their stories to the police."

Heart in her throat, Brenna managed a nod, trying to hide her trembling. Though hunters by nature, her people did not believe in mindless violence or senseless slaughter.

Two uniformed locals intercepted them.

"DEA," Carson said again, touching the brim of his cap. They looked at Brenna, eyed her jacket and relaxed their stances. One, a younger man, met her gaze and blanched. Some humans always reacted so to one of the Pack.

"Where's the FBI?" the shorter of the two officers asked, his tone disapproving. At Carson's shrug, he grimaced and moved aside to allow them access to the witnesses.

Striding across the room as if they belonged, they moved into the edge of the group surrounding the survivors.

Then she smelled it, mingled with the acrid, coppery scent of blood. His scent—faint, but definitely Alex. She felt an instant of panic. Was he hurt? She nearly turned to Carson, then, remembering he was not like her, glanced casually around the room instead.

There. A faded jean jacket lay crumpled on the floor next to the wall, splattered with blood. It carried her brother's scent. She would have to inspect it, smell it better and touch the cloth before she could determine if the blood belonged to him.

Carson's hand on her shoulder kept her in place.

An older, heavyset woman, bright spots of color high on her pale cheeks, talked quietly. "The leader was a tall man, built like a wrestler or something. Muscular, and he liked to show those muscles off, I think. Despite the weather, he didn't wear a shirt or coat, only a black leather vest. And jeans."

The officer taking notes nodded. "Any other distinguishing characteristics, ma'am?"

"His hair was long—longer than mine. Oh—and he had a tattoo."

Carson looked at Brenna. She knew he was thinking of Alex's birthmark, shaped like a wolf.

"Tattoo?" she asked, keeping her voice professionally level. "What did it look like?"

Eyes wide, the woman waved one plump beringed hand. "Oh, it was very intricate, some sort of curly snake thing, evil looking, that wrapped all the way up his arm."

Not Alex's birthmark. With an effort, Brenna kept her relief from showing on her face.

"Hades' Claws." One of the troopers muttered to another. "It's their mark."

Carson gave Brenna a narrow-eyed look, and she saw that he already knew about this tattoo. Again she wanted to open her mouth, to tell him Alex would never defile himself like that, but too many others surrounded them, so she held her silence.

"Eye color? Hair color?"

Ah, now was the important part. Brenna held her breath.

The woman didn't hesitate. "Dark eyes. Brown, I think. And that hair, why it was so inky black it didn't reflect the light. It had to be dyed."

Another officer had begun to question two more

tellers, who responded with similar answers to the first. Carson watched and listened, intent on their answers.

Brenna had heard enough. Glancing around the brightly lit interior of the bank, she wondered at the creepy feel of it, as though the room had taken on a texture both clean and sharp, yet tainted and foul. She ran her hand along the faux wood surface of a desk, the smoothness an odd contrast to the rough menace that still hung in the air.

Moving as unobtrusively as possible, she went to the jacket and lifted it, resisting the urge to bury her nose in the cloth and breathe in the familiar scent. Carson made no move to stop her, though she could feel his watchful gaze boring into her back. Instead she held the coat a few feet away, inhaled deeply and breathed.

Another's smell tainted the material, mingling with and overriding her brother's. This other man, a human who had left the sharp smell of anger and fear embedded in the fabric, had worn it recently. Though it might once have belonged to Alex, someone else had worn it here. With a quiet sigh, she let it fall back to the floor and turned to rejoin Carson.

Something else… Teasing her sensitive nose, the scent came strong, alive instead of dead. Not human nor of the Pack. She stopped before reaching Carson, carefully looking around. A high-pitched whimper from under a nearby desk caught her attention. Crouching down to peer underneath, she let her breath out in a quiet hiss. A tiny black puppy of mixed heritage, eyes huge and frightened, stared up at her from the floor, shaking.

Here, then, was something she understood, one in

many ways closer to her kind than the myriad assortment of humans inside this place. Still kneeling, Brenna held out her hand, letting the small creature absorb her scent before she reached out to stroke the softness of his midnight-colored fur, noticing the contrast of his white paws.

Touching the animal, Brenna felt a sensation of noise and terror. She shivered with the aftershocks of what the small creature had experienced and even now still felt. This young dog had been with his human companion when he died. Glancing at the sheeted bodies, she received a brief image of love, burst apart by a single gunshot to the head. The noise, the blood, the hatred, had terrified this young animal. Grieving and fearful, he was alone now.

Without a second thought, Brenna scooped him up in her arms. "I will be your protector now, small one," she promised, whispering the ancient words that had always bound her people to their animal companions.

"Has anyone viewed the tapes?" Carson asked the nearest officer.

"Not yet." The cop indicated another man, a plainclothes detective from the looks of him. "We were waiting for him."

"He's here, let's go," Carson barked.

The other two men conferred, then moved toward a darkened back office. Carson signaled Brenna to follow. Head held high, she did, the pup cradled in her arms, trying to burrow under her jacket.

"Where'd that dog come from?" one of the local officers asked, eyeing her suspiciously.

She lifted her chin to reply. "He was under the

desk. I think he might have belonged to one of the victims.''

The officer gave her a skeptical frown. ''Do they allow pets in here?''

''Who cares?'' the detective snapped. ''Let's go.''

With the lights dimmed, they had already set up the equipment to play the security tape.

''Ready?'' At the collective nod, he hit Play. Grainy images began to move on the monitor as the horrifyingly brutal robbery was reenacted in black-and-white.

From the general area outside the office, Brenna could hear a woman sobbing.

''There.'' One officer pointed to the tallest man in the video, the obvious leader, the one with the bare chest and intricate tattoo twining up his muscular arm.

''Can't see his face,'' another man grunted, leaning so close to the monitor his nose touched it.

A grumbled complaint from the others moved him back.

Brenna held her breath, letting it out with a loud sound as she got a better look at the criminals' leader. He was built like her brother, yes. But there the resemblance ended. Though she couldn't make out the killer's features, she could tell from the way the man moved that he was not her twin.

Relief flooded her. Carson's unwavering certainty that her brother had gone bad had given her doubts. But the man in the video was not Alex. A quick glance at Carson told her he knew that, as well.

''Hey.'' Catching the interaction, the detective moved closer. ''Why didn't you come with the other DEA guys who called this morning? They're on their way in.''

Carson went still. "We wanted to be first," he said. "We wanted to check around on our own."

Though the other man nodded, Brenna got the distinct impression he knew Carson was lying.

"As a matter of fact, I think we're gonna head into Hawks Falls and look around there. We'll check back with you guys tomorrow to see if anything new turns up."

As they left the room, Brenna heard one man comment, "DEA or FBI, they're all the same. Always want to sweep in and steal the glory, even from their own."

"What was that all about?" she asked, as soon as they were outside. "Why *aren't* you working with the other DEA guys?"

He didn't answer, just yanked her truck door open with a brusque motion. Without protest, she climbed into the cab, the puppy still tucked in the curve of her arm.

"Just a minute." Carson indicated the young dog with a wave of his hand. "Leave the animal here."

"No. That's not negotiable. He comes with me or I don't go at all."

Carson frowned. "That puppy doesn't belong to you."

"He does now." She pulled the door closed behind her with a thunk. Adjusting her seat belt, she made sure the dog was comfortable before turning to look at Carson, who was still standing outside the truck. Finally, as she continued petting the pup's soft fur, Carson shook his head and strode around the vehicle. He climbed into the driver's seat and slammed his own door. Without another word, he started the ignition and put the vehicle in Reverse.

"Tell me one thing," he said, one arm draped over the back of the seat. "Are you bringing that dog because he's your brother's?"

Brenna laughed. "You really think Alex would bring a puppy with him to rob a bank and kill a bunch of people? And then leave his pet behind?"

Carson lifted one shoulder in a shrug. "Why not?

In his tone she heard what he did not say: If The Wolf didn't value human life, what would the life of one small animal matter?

"Not my brother's," she told him finally. "I think the owner was probably one of the people killed in the robbery. Now it's your turn to answer a question. Why aren't you working with the other DEA agents? You lied. You didn't even know they were coming."

Carson drove as if a demon were chasing him, rapidly increasing their speed until they were hurtling down the highway. They took the left lane by storm and passed every other vehicle they encountered.

"What are you hiding?" Brenna heard the taunt in her voice and lifted her chin. "Tell me, Mr. Level-With-Me. Why aren't you working with the other government people?"

"I work better alone," Carson snapped. "I'll find him and bring him in before they even get their heads out of their asses."

"You never stop, do you?"

His expression grim, he shook his head. "No. And I never will. Not until he's in custody."

"Did it ever occur to you that he might still be undercover?"

"Yeah." His mouth twisted. "It did. Briefly. But I saw him. I'll never forget that. He shot my family, then threw away the gun. And he never contacted me.

Ever. Not even the day of the funeral, the day I buried Julie and Becky. He was my partner, damn it. My friend.''

The bitterness of betrayal rang in his voice. Unable to take the stark desolation in his eyes, she looked away.

''That wasn't Alex in the video,'' he said finally. He eased up on the gas pedal and moved into the middle lane.

Staring at him, she nodded. ''I know.''

''That doesn't mean he wasn't involved.''

''He wasn't.''

The puppy whimpered, shifting in her arms. Some of her tension must have communicated itself to the animal. Taking a deep breath, Brenna forced herself to relax.

''You'll see,'' she told him. ''Once we find him, I'm sure he'll have a reasonable explanation for everything.''

Ignoring her, Carson exited the freeway and pulled into a service station.

While he refueled, Brenna concentrated on her new companion. He had to have a name. For now she would call him Phelan, little wolf.

As she spoke the name out loud, three times in the custom of her people, the puppy raised his head. He lifted a small foot, accepting the naming with quiet dignity. As she took his paw in her hand, Brenna saw a splotch of rust marring the white fur. Blood, dried and flaking. Surely Carson had tissues or something in the glove box. A sidelong glance showed her that he had his back to her.

She opened the glove box. Inside there were no tissues, only a few sheets of paper, crumpled and wadded into a ball. One of those would have to do. Smoothing one out, she glanced at the words printed on it and froze.

"Leave of Absence—Medical." Swiftly she scanned the rest of the document. In disbelief she read it again, before crumpling and tossing the paper back. Carson Turner had lied. Whatever he did, he was no longer acting under the auspices of the DEA. Since early summer, he'd been on forced medical leave. Six months ago. That meant that in his hunt for her brother, he was acting alone and unsanctioned, his reasons personal rather than official.

A private vendetta. Now, more than ever, she knew she had to find Alex first.

Chapter 4

Outside, the sharp ice of the wind cut straight to the bone. Shivering, Carson regretted giving Brenna his work jacket. Quickly he fitted the icy gas nozzle into his tank, setting the metal pin so the gas would run automatically. Then, turning his back to the wind, he punched a number into his cell phone. Warm as it was inside the Tahoe, he needed to talk to his informant privately yet still keep an eye on his reluctant passenger.

Three rings, a click, then a muffled answer. As usual, the man he knew only as Jack didn't want to talk. Carson kept his voice low, rational, cajoling. He did the usual song and dance with the normal promise of payment, and finally got the information he needed. A potential sighting of Hades' Claws. As he'd thought they might, they were heading north, toward their compound in Hawk's Falls.

Jack believed Alex traveled with them.

Snapping the cell phone closed, he got back in the truck, shivering, and turned up the heat. A quick look at Brenna told him something had happened in the brief time he had taken to make the call. Her entire demeanor, posture and expression had changed. From the rigid line of her back to the way the sharp edge of her glare touched on him before skittering away, he read a simmering anger.

He swept the gas station at a glance. Two or three other vehicles were parked at the pumps, their drivers bundled against the cold while pumping gas. Nothing seemed out of the ordinary, and no one had approached the Tahoe while he was on the phone.

Then why was his new companion spoiling for a fight?

"What's up?" He avoided her gaze as he turned the key and started the engine. The less eye contact, the less chance for an argument.

"You used your cell phone. Who'd you call?" Her tone sounded surprisingly pleasant, even with contained anger.

He suppressed a smile. Damn she was good. Answering a question with another question. One of the oldest avoidance tactics in the book.

"Informant." Signaling, he pulled onto the road. With one hand looped over the top of the steering wheel, he fiddled with the radio, finding a station that played soothing classical music to calm her. Small tricks like that had become ingrained, something he did without conscious thought.

Her face still averted, Brenna made a sound low in her throat. It could have been either pleasure or disgust; he didn't know her well enough to determine which.

Nor did he care. Again he reached for the radio. One flick of the dial increased the volume to a level loud enough to discourage conversation, and he settled back in anticipation of a nice, quiet ride. Alex's sister seemed inclined to cooperate, watching the snow-covered landscape go past with no attempt to speak further.

But when the melody on the radio switched to Liszt's "Hungarian Fantasy," she swung around in her seat to face him. The swiftness of her movement, in keeping with the ominous crash of the music, startled him.

Even more alarming was her degree of anger. One quick glance told him the shoulder restraint was all that kept her from launching herself at him. Even her exotic eyes glowed caramel with fury. She took a deep breath, baring her white teeth, before exhaling loudly.

She looked almost like a wild animal.

"What the h—" Imagination. Had to be. He took a deep breath himself, blinked and took another look.

The furious glare remained. Quickly he turned the radio off.

"Now what?" he asked. "You got a problem?"

"Why did you lie to me?" Simmering rage trembled in her voice. "You said you had an official reason for looking for my brother, but you're not even working for the DEA."

Damn. He shook his head. "You snooped in my glove box."

"I was looking for a tissue. Instead I found a crumpled piece of paper that says you're on medical leave."

He clenched his jaw. "None of this is your business."

"I think it is." She tilted her chin, contempt blazing from her gaze. "Tell me, Carson Turner, have you become the thing you profess to hate?"

"What?"

"A criminal."

"Lady, I'm no criminal."

Again she blew out her breath. "You're acting without the sanction of the Justice Department. You're on medical leave. Impersonating a federal agent is a crime."

"You just did the same thing at the bank."

"That was different. You led me to believe you were there on official business, and I was with you. You've been doing it for...what? The last six months?"

Carson felt his face heat. "I have good reason—"

"Sure you do." Scorn sharpened her tone. "Even Ted Bundy thought he had good reason."

"Give me a break." He ran his hand through his hair, his earlier expectation of a peaceful drive evaporating. "You can't compare me to him."

"Why not? He's a murderer. You could be. Do you intend to kill my brother?"

A low growl rose in his throat. It sounded enough like an animal to cause the puppy to raise his head from Brenna's lap.

Oddly enough, Brenna smiled as though she found comfort in the sound.

"I'll bring The Wolf to justice. By whatever means necessary."

Brenna forced her jaw to relax. She would simply

have to wait and see what other lies he might have told.

Carson turned his head, looking directly at her for the first time in what seemed like hours. Holding his gaze, she resisted the strange, shivery sensation she got whenever their eyes connected. She didn't know if it was because of the threat this human represented or some other, inexplicable reason. Whatever the cause, she didn't like the feeling. She focused on the threat.

"I will not let you harm Alex."

His lips twisted into a mocking smile. "Hmm."

Brenna let that pass. Carson had no idea what he was dealing with. Most men took one look into her eyes and knew better than to toy with her. "Why aren't you afraid of me?"

He laughed. "Should I be?"

She tried a different tack. "Are you afraid of anything?"

Instantly he sobered. "I told you. I live for one thing only. Finding the people who destroyed my life and making them pay. Nothing and no one can keep me from that goal."

Back to that. Fine. "You want answers, right?"

"I want the truth."

"Then we're on the same side."

He quirked a brow in question, alternating his attention between her and the road. "How do you figure?"

"We both want facts."

"Yeah." A shadow of savagery remained in his tone. "That's why we're heading toward the Vermont border."

All right, she would bite. "Why? What'd you find out?"

"My informant told me that Hades' Claws is having a big meeting. Hundreds are assembling in a week's time in a place they have north of Hawk's Falls."

"How do you know you can trust him?"

"Trust who?"

"The informant."

"I've worked with him before. His tips have always panned out. As long as I pay, he tells me the truth."

"I thought you didn't pay for information," she said.

"Seldom." He smiled. "Sometimes I bluff."

"And if you don't pay?"

"Then he'd sooner let me die."

For some reason that touched her. "You live a sad life, Carson Turner."

His expression froze, the falsely pleasant mask slipping slightly to reveal hard ruthlessness underneath.

"Sad?" He shook his head. "Angry, maybe. Mad. Oh yeah, definitely furious. But not sad, not anymore. Not ever again."

She saw that her words had hit some deeply hidden mark. "I meant," she said, "it's sad that you have to pay people to help you."

He shrugged, a quick jerk of his shoulders. "Not in my line of work."

"And this?" With her hand she indicated the road ahead. "Is all this work, too? Pretending to be an active DEA agent, lying to other law enforcement guys, making me a captive?"

Holding her breath, she waited to hear his answer.

Though he'd lied to her initially, since she'd caught and confronted him, perhaps now he would tell her the truth.

"This is my life," he said, after a long silence. "Finding Alex, finding *them*, keeps me alive."

"Vengeance?"

He nodded.

Bleakness settled in her chest, icier than any northern blizzard. "You do mean to kill him."

"Maybe. I don't know. If he was the one—"

"If?" She pounced on the word. "You have doubts then?"

He continued as if he hadn't heard her. "If he was the one who betrayed me—us—and had Julie and Becky killed, he deserves to die."

She seized on the word. "'If.' You said if again."

"I saw him, Brenna."

"No." She remembered his exact words as clearly as if she'd written them down. "You said you saw him with a gun. But you never saw him shoot, did you?"

"Semantics," he snarled. "It's not like he tried to help me, now is it?"

"And you have the right to be his judge and his jury?"

"The right?" Raw savagery burned in his expression, from the hard set of his chin to his burning gaze. "I lost any rights long ago. I should have been the one to die, not my family. They were blameless, damn it. It was because of me, because of my job. They died without warning, without protection. They'd done nothing—" His voice broke, and he swallowed. White-knuckled, his hands gripped the steering wheel while he struggled to regain control of his emotions.

Such pain. Raw anguish. As quickly as it had begun, her protective anger faded. What must it have been like to lose everyone he loved? Brenna could only imagine.

"What about your parents?"

He continued to stare straight ahead. "What about them?"

"I imagine they care what happens to you."

"Imagine all you want. They're divorced. My mother lives in Seattle. She calls me once in a while, or I call her."

"Your father?"

He made a rude sound. "Remarried. New family. He doesn't need any of this."

"Any brothers or sisters?"

"Look, what is this?" His gaze raked her before he turned his attention back to the road. "Why are you asking so many questions? Why does any of this matter to you?"

His reaction stung. "I'm trying to figure you out, that's all."

"Well, stop. All the relatives in the world can't make up for the loss of my wife and daughter."

"I didn't think they could," she said softly. "But having them to depend on sure helps."

"Like you depend on Alex?"

She ignored the mockery in his tone. "Yes, exactly. Like I depend on Alex."

"I wouldn't depend on him too much. Looks like he ducked out on you, too."

She heard the unspoken: *like he ducked out on me.*

Though she tried to tear herself away, she found her gaze drawn to him. Despite the painful emotions still plain in the hard cast of his features, he handled the Tahoe with deft precision, moving in and out of lanes with the confidence of a skilled driver. His law enforcement training, no doubt.

Watching him channel his agony into driving, Brenna knew Carson meant what he said. The more she learned about him, the more she realized he wanted the truth and meant to find it, no matter what. This man took no half measures. He would be absolutely certain he had the right person before he started any course of action. Given that, she couldn't blame him for wanting to find her brother.

A thought struck her so hard that for a moment she couldn't catch her breath. What if Carson was right? What if her brother *had* been the one who'd murdered Carson's family? Just thinking such a thing felt disloyal and impossible, yet...

The evidence seemed damning. Carson himself had seen Alex with the gun. He was still involved with the biker gang. If he wasn't undercover, why was he with them? There had to be some sort of rational explanation.

"I don't understand why Alex hasn't contacted you," she mused. "Unless he's in danger."

"Because he's guilty." After a quick glance at her face, his tone softened. "Believe me, that's something I've wondered, too. Hell, Julie loved him like a brother. Becky called him Uncle. And he was my best friend."

Was. Once again, past tense. Did Carson see no possibility that he might be wrong? That someone else might have killed his family?

"When I was lying on the floor bleeding, I raised my head and looked at him. He knows I saw him. That's why he's trying to have me killed."

Brenna started. Though he spoke without inflection, she heard no doubt in Carson's voice. He truly believed that Alex... She couldn't complete the thought.

Again Phelan whimpered, shifting in her arms. Instantly she stilled her heart rate. She didn't want to alarm the puppy. In a moment he snuggled into her warmth, drifting back into a fitful doze.

"You should have let him out when we got gas," Carson commented. Since he was right, Brenna merely nodded.

With the radio off, the ebb and flow of traffic combined with the Tahoe's engine in a soft roar. Twice Brenna's eyes drifted closed. Both times she forced herself to sit up and stretch her neck and shoulders.

"How much longer will it take to get there?" she asked, not from any real need for conversation, but merely to break the silence and stay awake.

"An hour, maybe less." From his terse response, she doubted he wanted to talk any more than she did. Tough. She had to prepare herself for the situation they were headed into.

"Tell me about Hawk's Falls. What kind of situation are we going to find?"

Another sidelong glance. "Dangerous. If Jack—my informant—is right, a lot of money and drugs are going to change hands in a couple of days. They're smart. The big rally is a cover. With hundreds of bikers in town, no one will be able to tell when the deal goes down."

"So the bikers will be on edge?"

"Only the ones involved. The rest of them will be too busy partying to pay attention to anything else."

She sighed. "What kind of place is this?"

"Hawk's Falls? Typical small town. I've been through it once or twice. Nothing exciting."

"Then why do they allow this biker gathering?"

"Hey." Amusement sparkled in his eyes. "Most bikers are decent people. Their money's as good as anyone else's."

"What are we going to do once we get there? Do you have a plan?"

"We?" Carson shook his head, still watching the highway.

Amused, Brenna hid her smile. "Yes, we. Unless you plan to tie me up and leave me in here."

"Don't tempt me." he growled, though the slight lift at the corner of his mouth told her he was joking. So the man *did* have a sense of humor.

"Seriously, what are we going to do?"

"We have to be careful. Once we get to Hawk's Falls, we're going to play it by ear."

"You don't have a plan."

"I have a plan." A quick grin came and went on his face. "I just don't know what it is yet."

"We'll look for my brother."

"No." No trace of a smile relieved the hard cast of his features now. "We most definitely will *not* be looking for Alex."

Brenna's breath caught in her throat. If he was still kidding, he had an odd sense of humor. "Why not?"

He shrugged. "Basically, you're my bait. I want him to come to us, but I don't want to alarm the entire gang. So we pretend we don't care. Keep things low key."

"Bait?" Her voice rose. "As in setting a trap?"

"I want to talk to your brother. I told you it would be dangerous."

She waved away his words. "I don't care about me. I want to make sure we don't put Alex in danger."

"Danger? He'll probably be surrounded by his cohorts. I doubt I could get close to him. I mean to force your brother to talk to me. Having you with me in the line of fire is the best way I can think of to make sure that happens. So, yes, you're my bait. We're going to go into downtown Hawk's Falls and pretend to enjoy each other's company."

That galled, too. "What's the point? If Alex wants to find us, he will. His tracking skills are excellent. I'd like to find him first."

"No." Impatience sounded in the gravelly timbre of his voice. "With so much going on, he'll be busy. Distracted. I need to get his attention. Having you with me should do it. I want him alone, not surrounded by his gang."

"Alone." Brenna repeated the one word that bothered her. "I won't let you hurt him."

"So you've said."

"Then—"

"Try and understand. I need to talk to him. I want him to look me in the eyes and tell me, in his own words, what happened that day. Why he was there, at my house, holding the gun. Why he shot."

"And then you'll kill him."

"I'd like to think I'm better than that. I'd like to think I'd see him arrested, make sure he stood trial."

"But you're not sure."

He met her gaze. "I don't know. If he was the one who killed my family…"

"If he's as evil as you seem to think, he'd shoot you first."

He lifted one shoulder. "Then I'd know, wouldn't I? But before I died, I'd make sure to take him with me."

His violent words echoed in the interior of the Tahoe. Or maybe, she reflected, they bounced off the walls of her bruised heart. Carson didn't really care whether he lived or died, as long as he found out the truth and exacted vengeance. Hell of a way for a man to live.

Why his pain touched her so deeply, she couldn't say. Yet one thing stood out in all he'd said. Despite his seemingly firm conviction, Carson still didn't really know the truth. Even she was beginning to wonder what exactly had happened that day.

But Alex was her twin. She knew him nearly as well as she knew herself. He would have an explanation for everything. And, unless the danger was too great, once he knew of her presence, Alex *would* find her. Even if he had to change to do so.

Phelan lifted his head, watching the exchange between them with interest. Now, apparently having decided he wanted to check Carson out more thoroughly, he wiggled from her lap and sank to his stomach. Sniffing furiously, he stretched his stubby little body until his neck was fully extended. Still unable to reach Carson over the console, he began a slow belly crawl up and over.

"Hey." Gently Carson pushed him away. "If you're gonna let that dog travel with us, keep it away from me."

Brenna gathered Phelan back in her lap, making quiet soothing sounds while she stroked his soft fur. She hadn't imagined the flash of panic on Carson's face when Phelan licked his hand. Carson had built such a wall around himself that he couldn't even let a puppy get close. Again she felt her chest tighten; again she forced the feeling away. She couldn't afford to let pity—or any other emotion—cloud her judgment where Carson was concerned.

She'd always been a sucker for the underdog. The forgotten ones, the quiet children who remained in the background while the others shone, the formerly beloved pets that waited, ignored, in some suburban backyard while the television inside the house blared.

Her first concern had to be for her brother, but she couldn't walk away until she knew Carson had his answers and maybe, finally, peace.

How stupid was that? Thoroughly annoyed with herself, Brenna crossed her arms and glared at her oblivious companion.

She let her gaze wander as her glare faded into a perusal. He was a fine-looking man. His shoulders pleasantly filled out his sweatshirt, and his muscular arms spoke of more than a passing interest in physical fitness. Dark, shaggy hair and craggy, masculine features combined with his lean, athletic build, making him the kind of man most women drooled over.

His scent pleased her, too. Before she thought better of it, Brenna inhaled. Masculine, crisp and slightly musky, he carried the enticing smell of one who would make an excellent mate—if he were a shapeshifter, that is, she added hurriedly to herself, not liking the direction her thoughts had been heading. Mate indeed! After what had happened in her one attempt to marry a human, Brenna definitely wasn't up to that kind of agony again. Ever.

"Are you done?" he drawled.

Her gaze flew to his face. "What?"

"I asked if you were finished looking me over like I was your next meal?"

Deliberately she smiled, showing her teeth. Some humans—no, most humans—recoiled instinctively when they saw her in predatory mode.

Carson simply stared back, unsmiling.

"Don't get any ideas," he said.

For a moment she couldn't understand his meaning. When she did, she felt her face color. Still, because she rarely backed down, she challenged him.

"What kind of ideas? Enlighten me."

Was it a trick of the light, or did his own tan complexion turn red? His sensual lips thinned, and his eyes turned flinty as he glared at her.

"You know exactly what I mean."

"No." She batted her eyelashes for good measure, ignoring the unaccustomed butterflies in her chest. "I don't. Really. What kind of ideas do you not want me to have?"

For a moment she thought he might cry uncle. But evidently Carson Turner, renegade DEA agent, was every bit as stubborn as she.

"Sex." He spoke crisply. "You looked me over like a woman with sex on her mind."

Sex. Him. Her. A tangle of bodies. Hot, passionate—no. He was wrong. She laughed, unable to keep from choking midway through.

Still, her best response had to be humor. A pitiful attempt at laughing off his right-on-target remark.

"Hey, it's been a long time." She tried for a teasing tone and found it.

The darkness in his eyes deepened. "Look, I admit you're an attractive woman. And it's been a long time for me, too." His husky voice did strange things to her insides. "But I loved my wife. I couldn't even think of anyone else that way—"

The cell phone rang, interrupting him. Unlike the sometimes annoying specialty rings some phones had, he'd chosen a plain, unvarnished tone. Somehow she wasn't surprised.

"Unidentified caller." He glanced at the silver faceplate where the caller ID showed. "Only a few people have this number. We'll finish this conversation later." He stabbed the On button. "Hello?"

Was that a threat or a promise? Brenna settled back in her seat, trying to sort out her confused reactions to him.

She could smell her own desire. Mingled with that, despite his words to the contrary, she could smell the heady scent of his.

Complications like this she did not need.

Though she tried, she couldn't make out the voice on the phone. Listening, Carson narrowed his eyes.

"Alex?" The single word was full of shock—and fury. "Alex, is that you?"

Chapter 5

Alex?

"Give me the phone." Grabbing for it and missing, Brenna clenched her jaw as Carson snapped the flip top closed.

"Damn," he swore.

"Was it him?"

"Yes." The grim set of Carson's mouth exposed his agitation. "I could barely hear him. He was whispering."

Whispering? "He must be in danger and trying not to be overheard."

"Damn." Carson cursed again. "I don't believe this."

"Tell me what he said."

With a savage flick of the turn signal, he moved the Tahoe into the middle lane. "He gave me an order, plain and simple. 'Get Brenna out of here.'"

Alex. Concerned about her welfare. How did he

even know she was here? Maybe by using the same internal sense that told her he was in danger.

"Did he say anything else?" Leaning forward, she watched while Carson focused intently on his driving, trying unsuccessfully to change lanes again, this time into an unbroken line of traffic. Finally he negotiated an opening in the right lane and moved over. Their speed was now barely sixty.

"We have to exit in a half mile," he said. "After this we'll take mostly back roads."

She waved his words away. "Carson! Did Alex say anything else?"

The look he shot her was dark. "Not much," he drawled. "I'll repeat it. 'If Brenna gets hurt, there will be hell to pay. Get her out of here. Now.'"

"He's worried about me. And not just because I'm traveling with you. Whatever he's involved in is dangerous," she said. "Was that it?"

His expression turned cold, watchful and alert. "Did you expect a personal message? Something in code?"

Suspicion tainted his voice and gaze, forcibly reminding her that they were still on opposite sides of the fence.

"No." She sighed, wishing Alex had thought to give her some sort of signal. "I would have thought you two had a code, since you did undercover work together."

Carson shook his head. "All field agents use abbreviated speech for emergencies. He didn't use it."

"Did he sound okay?"

Carson made a sound of disgust. "Hard to tell from a whisper."

Phelan whimpered and lifted his small head to peer

up at her. Absently she stroked his soft fur. What kind of trouble was her brother in? Bad enough that he didn't want her anywhere near him, even though they both could change for protection.

"I don't get this." Speaking her thoughts aloud, she looked at Carson. "How long have you had that cell phone?"

"A couple of years. Why?"

"Because Alex still remembers your number. I don't understand why he hasn't contacted you before now."

"Here we are." Ignoring her, Carson jabbed his thumb toward the exit sign. Behind a beat-up, dirty, white panel truck, they slowed to nearly forty miles per hour.

"Come on." He drummed his fingers on the steering wheel. "We haven't got all day."

Brenna bit back a flash of anger. "Carson? Any thoughts? Why do you think Alex never called you?"

"Importance." He ground the word out between his teeth. "Until now he obviously didn't feel anything was important enough to merit a call."

The unsaid words hovered in the air. *Even when my wife and daughter were murdered and my world ripped apart. Even then his partner and former best friend hadn't called.*

She fought rising panic. "Something is terribly wrong."

Carson snorted. "You think?"

Without thinking, she placed her hand on his forearm and felt his muscles tense at her touch.

"I know my brother. If he called you his friend, he wouldn't rest until he helped you."

With a deft motion he shook off her hand and

drove. Now the road curved sharply, and the panel truck in front of them slowed further. Carson muttered under his breath.

They passed a weathered wooden sign. ''Welcome to Hawk's Falls. Population 1,240.''

''Twelve hundred and forty?''

''Yeah.''

''It *is* a small town. That's weird.''

''I know. You would think that would make them more obvious. But most of this area is rural wilderness. People mind their own business here.''

After the curve, the road widened to four lanes, with a concrete median. The panel truck remained on the left. Carson swung around to pass on the right.

''Damn idiot is speeding up.''

It was true. As they drew abreast of the dirty, unmarked truck, the driver matched his speed to theirs. Alongside them, the truck rattled and bumped as it kept pace.

''What's up with that?'' She envisioned men leaping from the van with machine guns spitting, just like in the movies. ''I don't like this.''

''Neither do I.'' Now Carson gripped the steering wheel with both hands, tension evident in the stiff set of his shoulders. ''They were behind us for miles on the interstate, then got in the right lane and wouldn't let us cut in front of them when it was time to exit. At first I thought they were following us—''

''Is it a government truck?''

''Maybe.'' Carson gunned the Tahoe, then eased off. A speed limit sign flashed past. ''These days, anything goes.''

''We're up to fifty-five, and the speed limit is forty

here," she said. She could practically taste his agitation. Or maybe that was merely her own.

"Yeah, there's one more sharp curve ahead, then it will be thirty, because we'll be downtown."

The white truck slowed to take the curve. As it did, it drifted across the solid line into their lane.

"Look out!"

Carson stomped on the brake, causing the Tahoe to fishtail. They missed clipping the truck's bumper by inches, coming to a sliding stop just behind it.

It proceeded on a few hundred feet, weaving across both lanes of the deserted road.

"Something—" Before he finished speaking, the truck swerved and came to a screeching halt, blocking both lanes completely.

"They're waiting for us." Jaw set, Carson put the Tahoe in Reverse. "We'd better get out of here."

"How? You can't see."

"I think I can."

"It's a blind curve. We'll be killed."

Two men dressed entirely in black jumped from the cab of the truck. Both carried shotguns.

Carson put the Tahoe in Drive. "You want to take your chances with them?"

Brenna sat up straight. "We can take them."

He stared hard at her. "Are you crazy? They have guns!"

She exhaled, forcing away the adrenaline pumping in her blood, hoping her eyes didn't show how badly she wanted to fight. "You're right, but I don't care. Let's go."

With a short bark of savage laughter, he gunned the engine. The Tahoe surged forward, directly at the gunmen. One of the men jumped to the side, out of their path. The other remained where he stood, cradling the gun—good, that meant he wouldn't shoot it. He lifted his arm to throw something.

"Get down!" Carson yelled.

Instantly, Brenna obeyed, dropping her head and touching her nose to her knees.

They bumped across the median and sped past on the wrong side of the road. As they did, the rear window shattered, showering her with glass.

"What the—"

"We're past them. We lucked out. No one was coming from the other direction." Carson sounded irrationally calm. Too composed. Still, she sensed his rage.

"Are they following us?"

He checked the rearview mirror. "No, they don't appear to be. Maybe they just wanted to scare the hell out of us."

"Did they shoot? Is that what broke the window?" Sitting up again, Brenna shook her head, sending tiny bits of glass flying. Gingerly she brushed herself off.

"No gunshots. That one guy threw something through the glass. You need to see what it is."

Brenna looked over her shoulder. A large brick covered in shards of glass rested on the back seat.

"A brick." She brushed more glass from the upholstery before leaning over the seat to retrieve it. "You'd think they could have been a little more creative. Look," she mocked. "There's even a note attached."

She lifted the brick and undid the rubber band holding a white piece of paper in place.

"A note?" Carson glanced at her, then back to the road. "Read it to me."

Carefully she unfolded the crumpled paper. Made from letters cut from a magazine and pasted on the page were two simple sentences, which she read aloud. "The Lamplight Motel, Hawk's Falls. Meet me there." At the bottom of the page, a name—The Wolf. Her brother's nickname.

"That doesn't make sense," she mused. "First he calls, warning us away, then uses goons to break your window to send a message asking us to meet him? No way."

"He's nuts."

Brenna sent him a savage look. "This note isn't from Alex. We're being set up. I think it's a trap."

"You do, do you?" Carson whistled, the sound causing Phelan to try to stand in her lap. "Still trying to protect him?"

"I don't get it. Protect him how?"

"You want me to think this rendezvous is a trap so I won't go to the Lamplight Motel. Then you can slip off and meet your brother without me."

This time Brenna laughed, a bit wildly, since adrenaline still coursed like a jolt of caffeine through her blood. "Get real. Why would Alex resort to such drastic action to send a simple message? For that matter, why would anyone?"

"Exactly." Carson narrowed his eyes. "But then, why would anyone kill my wife and daughter?"

Carson snapped his fingers. "Bingo. I know why. He's insane."

Brenna bit her lip. None of this made sense. Alex wasn't a criminal, nor was he crazy. She knew him better than anyone, Carson included. If only he would *talk* to her, she knew she would get to the bottom of things.

Like why he'd never contacted Carson.

Someone else was involved, thus the old-fashioned, heavy-handed brick through the window. But who? Most likely the same people who wanted to kill Carson.

Glancing up, she saw the dense undergrowth in the trees had thinned out. They went around another bend in the road. Myriad brick buildings, many of them restored, decorated the outskirts of the town.

"Here we are," he said. "Hawk's Falls. Now we need to find the Lamplight Motel and check in."

Brenna stared. "Look, Carson. While I can take care of myself, I don't know if I can protect you. I *know* this is a trap. If Alex truly wanted to meet me somewhere, he'd make sure I knew without a doubt the message was from him. And he wouldn't sign the note The Wolf."

"Does insanity run in your family?"

For a moment she only gaped at him. "What?"

"Look at you. What are you, five feet tall?"

"Five-one."

"And I'll bet you're a hundred pounds, soaking wet."

"So?"

"You really think you can protect yourself from these people?" His tone left no doubt what he thought of that.

"I'm tougher than I look. But like I said, I don't know that I can protect you."

"Is that a threat?"

"No." She sighed. "Just the truth. The letter isn't from Alex. You say people are trying to kill you. I think they're setting a trap. I can't protect you from guns."

"You can't protect me from guns." His cool tone indicated his disbelief. "You're as bad as he is. What kind of life do you people lead?"

"I'm trained in martial arts."

He glanced at her sideways. "Martial arts, right. What exactly do you do for a living?"

"I'm a librarian." She grinned. "I live upstate, in a small town called Leaning Tree."

"For a librarian you have strange hobbies," he said.

"Jujitsu classes were Alex's idea. He wanted me to be able to protect myself. Always."

She glanced at him. Anger simmered underneath his skin, radiating from him. Furious, he looked deadly, like one of the lead hunters in the Pack. Again she felt an unwelcome tug of sexual attraction.

"You're lying." He made a sound of frustration. "You know more than you're saying."

Instead of responding, she studied the town. Hawk's Falls was a charming place, with neat, well-tended buildings and a quaint air. Small-town America at its best.

"I can't see why a biker gang wants to meet here," she said.

"Changing the subject?"

"I've told you everything I know," she said.

"I'll let it go. For now."

"Good." She lifted her chin, daring him to accuse her again of lying. "Now tell me why this biker gang would want to congregate here."

"Their leader, a guy named Nemo, has a farm north of town. Over a hundred acres, isolated and fenced."

The name took her by surprise. "Nemo? Like in *Twenty-Thousand Leagues under the Sea?*"

"Yeah." One corner of his mouth lifted. "Kind of sappy for such a dangerous man. He's deadly, though, make no mistake about it. I met him when Alex and I were undercover." A pained expression crossed his face, and whatever else he'd been about to say died.

"There." He pointed. "The Lamplight Motel."

A weathered sign hung from a seven-foot-tall, black cast-iron lantern. At the end of the cracked blacktop drive, the motel itself had been painted a cheery yellow.

Brenna sighed. "Here we go again. Two rooms?"

"One."

He still didn't trust her. "Fine."

After they were settled in their room, which this time smelled blessedly free of stale cigarette smoke, Brenna began to pace. It had been a while since she'd changed, and she was beginning to feel the need. Since she couldn't, she needed to do something else to dispel her nervous energy. A two-mile jog sounded wonderful, but she doubted Carson would go for it. Still, the outdoors beckoned.

"I need to go for a walk." Crossing her arms, she gave him a look that left no room for argument. "You can come with me or not. I don't care. But I'm going. I need exercise."

On the floor near her feet, Phelan cocked his head. He whimpered and pawed at her leg, tongue lolling.

"He needs a walk, too." Without waiting for Carson's response, Brenna picked up the puppy and headed for the door.

"Wait. I'm coming with you."

Hand on the knob, she paused. "Well, come on, then."

"Don't you want this?" Her coat dangled from his hand. "It's twenty-seven degrees. The wind chill is probably in the teens."

A coat. Brenna had nearly forgotten. She seldom wore jackets unless the temperature dipped far below freezing, as her internal body heat was much higher than a normal human's. That enabled her to stay warm even in subzero temperatures.

"Here." He tossed it to her. "I brought it in. I thought you might need it."

"Thanks." After placing Phelan on the bed, she slipped it on, leaving the zipper undone. Then she scooped up the puppy and stepped out, lifting her face to the cold slap of the chill breeze.

The air contained the scent of snow. The wind blew crisp and exhilarating, beckoning to her to enjoy winter, her favorite season. She increased her pace, heading for the fringe of trees to the west.

"God, I hate winter." Beside her, Carson turned up his collar. "That wind cuts like a knife."

Ignoring him, Brenna continued to scent the air. No danger here—yet. Only the chill sharpness of winter and the silent call of the woods. Exhilarating. The longing to change, to run as a wolf, shook her. All that she was, her very nature, seemed contained in this slight expanse of forest. Here she belonged. Still, she must remain human for now. She suppressed the urge to change, pushing it deep inside herself.

Phelan squirmed in her arms, feeling the pull of nature just as she did. Stooping, she let him loose, watching with envy as he romped and rolled in the snow. If she were free to change she would join him, frolicking without a care.

"Keep one eye open," Carson said, his voice low. "If they've been tracking us, we'll be an easy shot out here, unprotected."

Brenna started. "What did you say?"

"We'll be an easy—"

"No. Before that."

"Keep one eye open?"

She jerked her head in a nod. "When I was a kid, my mother used to put it a different way. 'Sleep with one eye open,' she always said."

With a puzzled look, he studied her. "Why would a mother say such a thing to a young child? Seems like it would scare the daylights out of you."

"It was meant to." Brenna laughed softly. "Who knew what kind of threats we might face?"

Carson stopped, frowning. Hunched against the cold, he had his hands in his pockets. "Where did you grow up?"

Guarded now, Brenna forced a smile. "Alex and I grew up on a farm upstate, near the Canadian border. Very remote and isolated. There were lots of wild animals and dangers you city folk never have to deal with."

Not entirely a lie. But the real danger always came from humans. Though members of the Pack integrated well, if humans were to discover the Pack's ability to shape-shift, they would panic and attempt to destroy them. Such a thing had happened before, long in the past. Because of that history, they always had to be guarded and abide by the unbreakable laws.

"Your brother never mentioned a farm." Though steady, Carson's tone sounded suspicious.

"Apparently Alex kept a lot of things to himself."
Though she meant to be flippant, her remark served
to remind both of them that perhaps she hadn't truly
known her brother at all.

"I know."

To the left, a twig snapped. Phelan barked, then set
off after the sound. Brenna jumped, even though she
still detected no danger. "Phelan!" she called, glancing at Carson, knowing if he weren't with her, she
would investigate herself.

"It might be a rabbit or a raccoon," Carson said,
his wide-legged stance reminding her again of an al-
pha male in the Pack.

"It might. But on the off chance that it's something
bigger, I want to keep the puppy near." She called
again.

"Good luck. If it's a deer, you'll never get him to
come."

"A deer," she repeated. *Prey.* Though she longed
to hunt, Brenna called Phelan a third time. This time
the young dog instantly obeyed, running full tilt until
he crashed into her leg. He sat expectantly in front of
her, tongue lolling, a blissful expression on his face.

"What the hell?" Narrow-eyed, Carson looked
from her to the dog and back to the woods. "How
did you make him do that?"

"Do what?"

"Come instantly when you called him? You
haven't had time to work with him."

"He's smart."

"Maybe. But still…"

She smiled. "It sounds like you know a lot about
dogs."

"Some." He looked away. "I…we used to have

one." He swallowed. Fascinated, Brenna watched the movement of his throat.

"Used to?"

"Yeah. His body was the first thing the responding officers found when they arrived on the scene. Cody died protecting my family." Hunching his shoulders, he turned away.

Her first instinct was to comfort him. But would he accept consolation from the sister of the man he believed responsible for so much pain?

"I'm sorry," she said instead, keeping her hands to herself.

His back to her, he made no response.

"I'm good with dogs." She began to speak, saying anything to distract him from his anguish. She rumpled her pup's fur. "Phelan understands me, and I understand him. Don't you, boy?"

Phelan grinned up at her. He knew what she was.

Turning, Carson looked at his watch. "How much longer do you need to walk?" His hawk-like features were once again expressionless. Rubbing his hands together, he blew on them. "It's colder than a well digger's butt out here."

Looking from him to the gray sky that still promised snow, then to the unexplored shadows of the woods, Brenna sighed. The powerful craving to shake off her human form, to change and run free, unbridled and unbound, still simmered in her blood. She actually trembled, so strongly did the desire consume her.

"See." Carson took her arm. "You're shivering."

For a moment she couldn't speak, afraid she would snarl or make some other nonhuman sound. She took a deep, shuddering breath, then another, watching the white plumes of frost hover in the air each time she exhaled.

When the longing decreased enough so that she felt human again, Brenna pulled her arm free.

"I could use—" Her voice broke. Clearing her throat, she tried again. "I could use something to eat."

Phelan barked. His intent gaze was focused on the woods.

Quickly, she picked up her puppy. He squirmed in protest and barked again, trying to lunge out of her arms.

Now the back of Brenna's neck tingled a clear warning. "Someone's there. Human, not animal."

Instantly Carson straightened. One hand slipped inside his jacket, and Brenna saw the glint of black metal holstered there.

"Let's go back to the motel." He kept his voice low. "I'm going to move close to you, for cover. Walk slowly, like you haven't noticed anything out of the ordinary."

Quieting the still-protesting Phelan with a sharp word, Brenna did as Carson asked. He moved in behind her, his broad shoulders effectively cutting out the wind.

Silently they retraced their tracks across the snowy field, then the parking lot. When they reached the door to their room, some of the tension left her shoulders. Phelan remained agitated, squirming in her arms.

Once inside, she let him go. He raced to the window, trying to see over the bulk of the heating unit and making little yapping sounds low in his throat.

"He saw something." Pulling off his jacket, Carson kept his holster on, gun in plain view.

"Whoever it was, he meant to harm us."

Suspicion caused Carson's expression to harden. "You know this because...?"

How to explain the sixth sense that kicked in whenever she was in danger? The warning had been clear, but not urgent. Brenna shrugged. "At least he didn't shoot at us."

"Did you expect him to?"

She squared her shoulders. "Could have."

"But didn't," Carson mused. Some of the hostility left his face. "Still, he didn't show himself, either. The note said he would contact us at the hotel. Here we are. Where's The Wolf?"

Sighing, Brenna removed her own parka. Already she felt too hot, with the heater blowing a steady stream of warm air. "I told you, that note's a fake. Alex didn't write it."

"Whoever did wants to meet. Maybe it's an informant." Carson shrugged.

"Or a killer. We need to take precautions," she said. "There's no sense in being sitting ducks."

His gaze sharpened. "Like we were a minute ago in the woods. Tell me, Brenna, was that deliberate? You wanted to go for a walk. Did you set me up?"

Biting back a sharp retort, she marched across the room and grabbed the plastic ice bucket. "You really are the most annoying man. I warned you out there. If I wanted to set you up, you'd be dead by now. I would have killed you myself."

"Are you going to throw that at me?" He indicated the ice bucket, one corner of his mouth lifting in the beginning of a smile.

She stared at him. At the bucket. Then she laughed. "No. We need ice. A couple of diet colas would be nice, too."

As he reached to take the bucket from her, the room phone rang. Brenna jumped, then looked at Carson. They both started for it at the same time.

Carson reached the phone first. Elbowing her out of the way, he plucked it from the receiver. He listened intently, then slammed the phone back in its cradle.

"Alex?"

He nodded. "Interesting. Now instead of just wanting you gone, I've been ordered to get myself the hell out of town, as well—and I have until midnight tonight to do it."

Brenna studied Carson's face. Judging from the muscle that jerked in his jaw, the call had infuriated him. "Or?"

"That's the thing." The bleak fury in his dark eyes froze her. "He knows there's nothing else he could do to me. So he's trying to bribe me instead. If I do as he asks, he says he'll turn himself over to me on Friday."

Chapter 6

He didn't know which pissed him off more—the fact that his former partner thought he was an idiot, or the utter lack of reaction with which Brenna took the news. Obviously, she still didn't believe her brother had become a vicious criminal. Talk about blinders.

"Why Friday?"

"It's the day after the big drug deal is supposed to happen."

"Tell me exactly what he said," she demanded.

Carson took a deep breath. Struggling to keep his voice flat and unemotional, he jammed his hands in his pockets and looked at the ceiling. "He repeated what he said earlier on my cell. 'Get Brenna out of here. I don't want her hurt. And I want you gone, too. Get out by midnight, before you get yourself killed. Don't mess this up for me.'"

"By midnight, huh?"

"Yeah. By midnight tonight." Carson ran a hand

through his hair. "Though, as threats go, it was pretty ineffectual. He didn't back it up with anything except his stupid promise. More than anyone, I know his word is no good."

"What else?" Determination colored her tone. "I need his exact words. Please."

Carson turned to study her. "'Tell Brenna I'm all right. But she has to leave right away. No ifs, ands or buts.'"

She sank down on the bed, relief, worry and joy all at once showing on her face. "Alex."

So much love in her voice when she said his name, Carson thought, infuriated. But he himself was alone in the world because of her brother, and that infuriated him even more. "What was that, some sort of code?"

"In a way. Our mother used that expression, too; just like keeping one eye open. Alex and I made fun of it our entire lives. He said it for me, so I would know without a doubt it was him."

"Yeah, well, your very considerate brother's been trying to kill me." He knew he sounded savage, and he felt absurdly guilty as he watched her smile vanish. "Does he really think I'll turn tail and run when I'm so close? Turn himself in on Friday—right."

"He's worried about your safety as well as mine." Brenna stood and crossed her arms. Worry darkened her eyes. "He has a reason for everything. I know he has."

"I'm not leaving," Carson said, dark promise making his voice nearly a growl. He could have softened it, but he wanted to make sure she understood he meant what he said.

"Neither am I." Now she wrapped her arms around

herself, in a hug. "Until I talk to Alex and find out the truth, I'm not going anywhere."

"I know." Feeling compelled by some strange impulse he didn't understand, in three steps Carson crossed the room to stand in front of her. Cupping her chin in his hand, he forced her to look up at him.

"As long as you're with me, he has to come to us. You're my insurance."

She stared at him, shock making her eyes widen. "You mean to use me against my brother?"

"I—" At first he thought she was trembling from fear. Then her gaze pinpointed on him, narrowing. Too late, he realized she was shaking not from fear but from anger.

He released her chin and stepped back.

"I shouldn't have said that," he admitted. "I just meant—"

She moved toward him. "You plan to use me to make Alex suffer."

"No." He meant it.

"It will never happen. I won't let you use me." The flat certainty in her tone both intrigued and infuriated him.

"What kind of monster do you think I am?" He turned away before she answered, telling himself he really didn't care, but still not willing to see the stark condemnation on her face.

"No more innocent lives will be lost because of me. I've got enough stains on my soul." He hadn't meant to reveal so much. Since he had, he might as well finish.

"I'm not like your brother."

"Listen to me." Moving silently, she came up behind him and placed her hand on his shoulder. He held himself still only by sheer effort of will. "You're a desperate man. I understand you want revenge. I'd want vengeance, too. But you've got to look for the truth in all this or else none of it will matter. You need justice, not a blind settling of scores."

His throat closed. Each word she spoke increased his confusion. How simple it had all seemed before he'd met her, when he'd been a hundred percent certain Alex had been the one who betrayed him and killed his family.

"I still think he did it," he muttered. He couldn't summon enough strength to brush her hand from his shoulder. Until now, until Brenna, he hadn't realized how much he craved human contact.

She squeezed. "But you're not positive."

His gut twisted. "No." The single word burst from him. "Because of you, now I'm not positive."

He heard her swift intake of breath and slowly turned to look at her. She let her hand fall. He wondered if he would see amusement or—God forbid— pity on her expressive face. But he saw only warmth and compassion, two things that had been absent from his life for so long.

Their gazes met. Locked and held.

"Brenna." He spoke her name as a warning.

She chose not to take it. With her chest nearly touching his, she gazed up at him, the obstinate tilt of her chin somehow endearing.

Maybe because she smelled of a long-forgotten spring, or because her soft mouth parted and her pupils darkened, or maybe because he just plain wanted to, Carson bent his head and kissed her.

After her first startled hiss of breath, she reached up and drew him closer. Her lips moved under his, unbelievably, delectably sweet. His body responded with a violence that stunned him. Desire slammed into him, heating his blood, thickening his body. Guilt—what the hell did he think he was doing?—surfaced, clawing at him. Out of reflex, he tried to picture his dead wife's face in his mind. That always brought him some measure of comfort.

But for the first time, he couldn't see her. He saw only Brenna, with her warm smile and freckled nose. Panic replaced craving. He pulled himself away, breaking the kiss and stepping from the intoxicating circle of her arms.

She, unlike the hell of his memories, let him go without a word.

Ignoring his body's insistent ache, he chose to focus on the smile that trembled at the corners of her mouth. How could she regard this kiss as somehow amusing, while to him it felt like the epitome of disloyalty.

"Another trick?" His voice dripped ice. He felt a pang as confusion clouded her eyes, but he pushed it away.

Meeting his gaze without guile, she combed through her hair with her fingers, mussing it in a way he knew was unconsciously sexy. "I won't bother to answer that," she said. "You're furious. With me or with yourself?"

He set his jaw and crossed his arms, feeling an absurd need for self-defense. "Sleeping with me won't help your brother."

"Sleeping with—" Lifting her hand as if to slap him, she apparently thought better of it and shook her head instead. The light went out of her lovely face. "You're crazy."

"Am I?" He should stop, he knew, but his guilt and the erratic beat of his heart goaded him on. "Then why did you kiss me?"

"I kissed you *back*." Scorn rang in her tone. "You initiated it."

Suddenly weary of the entire thing, he turned away.

"I'm a fool," he said. Crossing to the small window, he lifted a corner of the curtain and peered outside. The parking lot was empty, and the late-afternoon sky once more threatened snow. The pewter of the sky matched his mood.

"Let's forget this ever happened," he told her, unable to keep the anger from his voice. Looking back over his shoulder at her, he saw that she was crouched on the floor, petting her small puppy's belly. The dog looked comical, all four paws in the air waving madly, tongue lolling to the side of his mouth. His eyes were closed, and he appeared to be grinning in sheer bliss.

Carson felt a pang. Both for what he'd lost and for what he would never have. For an instant he could imagine her hands touching him, stroking, sensual...

No. No more mindless lust. He forced himself to remember. Doing so would bring back the pain, then the welcome numbness that had turned his world to gray. Damn Brenna for even thinking she could make him feel.

Movement outside captured his attention. A man, dressed in a nondescript black overcoat, crossed to the room alongside theirs. Though he kept his head down, his pace unhurried, the way he moved was as familiar to Carson as the generic dark blue or black car he bet the man drove. If one was here, there were always others. Carson would bet his last dollar that federal agents were their neighbors, though whether FBI or DEA, he didn't know.

Either way, since his supervisor had already warned him off this investigation, it didn't look good for him. If they saw him, they would consider him a rogue and place him under arrest.

Once more the stakes had been raised. Not only did he have to keep himself and Brenna alive, but he also had to remain invisible to the Feds.

Another thought occurred to him. If federal agents were converging here, his informant had been right. Something big was going to happen in Hawk's Falls in a couple of days. Perfect. Maybe Hades' Claws—and Alex—would be too preoccupied to make any more attempts on his life.

Though he wouldn't bet on it.

"What is it?" She reached him, moving in that soundless way of hers that would be an asset in his line of work. Right now he found it a liability.

He turned abruptly, blocking the window. "Just the people in the room next door."

"Oh," she said.

"Were you expecting Alex?" With an effort of will, he kept himself from glancing back outside. "I thought you didn't expect him to show up here."

The disgusted look she gave him nearly made him laugh. "I don't. If Alex could come to me, he would."

"Such faith," he mocked. "I used to trust him like that, too. But now I know better."

She smiled. "Tell me about what it was like when he was your partner."

For a moment he was so dumbfounded that he couldn't speak. His chest suddenly felt tight with too

many memories: Alex playing with Becky, bringing
her a huge, floppy rag doll—her first. Alex at his dinner table, joking with Julie over pot roast, helping
with the dishes. Drinking Bud Light and munching
on pizza while the two of them watched football. Alex
always cheered for the Vikings while he rooted for
the Giants. Now the memories felt like quicksand,
dragging him down.

"No," Carson said. "I'd rather *you* tell *me* about
him." At her startled look, he elaborated. "About his
life before I knew him."

As she watched him, her smile broadened. "Only
if you return the favor later. I want to know about
when he was your partner. He never told me about
any of that. His degree was in marketing."

"I used to tease him about that." The words
slipped from him before he thought better of it. "At
least I knew about his marketing degree."

"There's so much he never told me." She sounded
so hurt that he felt an impulse to comfort her. Knowing how easily one touch could lead to folly, he suppressed it. Instead, he twisted his mouth in what he
hoped would pass for a smile.

"I know."

She sat down on the edge of her bed, still watching
him with a thoughtful expression. "What exactly did
you want to know?"

How could he answer, when he didn't really know
the answer himself? Why even try to understand the
man who'd been like a brother to him, then betrayed
him so horribly? Yet how many sleepless nights had
he paced, trying to do exactly that? To understand the
why of it?

He glanced at her, at Alex's sister, the woman who

still believed in fairy tales. She couldn't begin to understand the depths of the horror he'd witnessed. Blood and death and evil were as foreign to her as love was now to him. She didn't belong here.

But love and worry for a brother who surely didn't deserve it, made her place her own life in danger.

Unabashedly he studied her. She met his gaze, the same intent look on her mobile features. He saw it now, the resemblance to his former partner, every so often when she turned her head a certain way or smiled at her puppy's playful antics. They had the same dark brown eyes. Their profiles were similar. But there the resemblance ended. Alex stood over six feet tall, while Brenna barely cleared five feet. Her hair was the color of sable, while Alex was blond. Brenna's bones were delicate, nearly fragile in appearance, while Alex had the lean, sturdy build of a fighting man.

"I want to know all of it." He cleared his throat. "Like I said, Alex never mentioned any family."

"He didn't have any family left, besides me. Our mother died when we were still teenagers." Her gaze never wavered from his face. "We were seventeen. After Mom passed away, all we had was each other."

"What about your father?"

She lifted one shoulder in a gesture he thought was meant to be a shrug that somehow fell short. "Who knows? We never knew him."

"So—"

Holding up her hand, she smiled. "My turn. Tell me when you first met Alex."

"Training." He thought back to that crisp autumn day. He'd been full of exuberance and naive hope. His dream job was finally within reach. "Like the FBI boys, we trained in Quantico, Virginia. Alex was in my class."

"I didn't even know," she marveled. "All he told me was that he had a new job. One he was excited about."

"Yeah." Carson tried not to remember how Alex had been the star of their class. His keen intelligence and enthusiasm had been contagious. The mysterious fascination women had for him was a plus for the guys who'd hung with him. "Women flocked to him."

Brenna laughed. "Even when he was a teenager, he had that problem. Though he did come to like it eventually."

"You must have had a similar reaction from guys." Carson hadn't meant to blurt those words, but he saw from the odd shadow that crossed her face that he'd touched on something sensitive.

"There weren't many guys," she said, drawing out the word as if she found it distasteful, "in the small town where I live. I was engaged once, but it didn't work out. I never went out into the world like Alex."

Out into the world. Odd choice of phrasing. He studied her face, looking for clues. Though he could have sworn he'd seen a brief flash of pain in her dark eyes, now her expression might have been carved in stone. He opened his mouth to ask his next question.

"Nope. My turn," she said. "I'm counting that as a question. Since Alex was your partner, exactly what kind of work did you do together?"

"Not office work," he shot back. "And I really didn't see my earlier remark as a question. It's still my turn. I want to know about this fiancé."

"Wait." The shadow had returned to her eyes, telling him that he hadn't imagined it. "I would rather not talk about him. He's…" She paused for so long that he began to imagine all sorts of crazy things to finish the sentence.

"He's what?" Carson cocked his head. "A biker? A cop? A—"

"He's dead," she said, her expression as bleak as he imagined his was when he talked about his lost family. A thousand other questions came to mind, first and foremost the need to know how he'd died, but Carson decided that could wait for another time. Asking her would have felt too much like tearing the wings off an innocent butterfly.

"And that's not about Alex. That's personal."

"You're right." He dragged his hand through his hair. "I don't know why I asked. It's none of my business. I'm sorry. Go ahead and interrogate me." He gave her a quick smile, meant to ease the sting of his word choice.

She nodded, relief lightening her gaze. "Okay, then, elaborate, please. You said you and Alex were in the field. You mentioned undercover work. Like police officers or what? Did you assume other identities, different names? What exactly did you do?"

"We were in the Drug Enforcement Agency." He emphasized the first word. "Our job was to find the people who transported and smuggled drugs. The big guys. We let the local police go after the small fish. And, yes, of course we had false names and identification."

She looked at him, chewing her bottom lip. Something still bothered her, and Carson thought he might know the reason.

"Did Alex do drugs?" she blurted. "Is that maybe why—"

He'd guessed correctly. "Not that I know of." He took another look at her face. Again he saw the quick flash of pain in her eyes. "Maybe why…what? Why he killed my family? Wait a minute. You believe me now?"

"I don't know what to believe."

He felt the oddest urge to comfort her. Though he couldn't pinpoint the exact moment when his own innocence had been destroyed, he knew he'd been a better man before. Now, not only was his innocence gone, but the very reason he had for drawing breath depended on gaining vengeance from the same man who'd had a part in ripping out his heart.

Carson began to pace, the hotel room suddenly seeming too small, too warm, too much like a trap.

"Believe this," he said, the words coming out raspy, instead of strong, as he'd intended. "Your brother is not the same person you knew. Sometimes when we work undercover—" he remembered the instructor's lessons in Quantico "—we run the danger of losing our original identity to the new one. Especially if that identity is more exciting, more dangerous. I think that's what might have happened to Alex."

"If that were true, Alex would have forgotten I existed. Obviously, he hasn't."

He gave a noncommittal nod, risking another quick look out the window. The courtyard now appeared deserted. The parking lot held only his Tahoe and the government-issue sedan.

"Carson?" Brenna's voice no longer sounded uncertain.

Turning, he saw she'd regained a bit of color in her face.

"How did you know Alex?"

Jamming his hands in his pockets, he forced himself to stand still. "We met at the academy. Why?"

"You knew him well?"

"I thought I did." He frowned. "But obviously I didn't."

"There has to be something," she persisted. "If you didn't see him shoot you or your family, you must have some other reason to make you suspect a man you once trusted."

"I have plenty of reasons."

"Pick one." Her tone dry, Brenna crossed her arms.

"I didn't see anyone else at my house that day."

"Were you shot first?"

Swallowing, he forced the word out. "Yes."

"Did you remain conscious?"

Now this was an interrogation. Though he didn't want to relive that day, he felt as if he owed Brenna the facts. After all, he was asking her to believe horrible things about her beloved brother.

"No. They—he—shot me in the back. I blacked out. When I came to, the rest was already over."

Her eyes looked huge. Once again her face had gone pale.

God help him, he couldn't move. Couldn't breathe, couldn't think. "Enough," he said. "No more."

She inhaled, her chest heaving. "I'm sorry. Let me ask this, then. Do you have any other reason to suspect my brother? Did his behavior change? Did he do anything that seemed weird?"

"Yes." Relief flooded him. Back on solid ground,

he could talk about anything but what had happened on that awful day. "Alex first started to change when his wife left him."

"Wife?" She looked blank. Stunned surprise? Her shock seemed genuine.

"How many sisters don't even know their brother has gotten married?" he drawled.

"He couldn't have. He would've told me."

Carson simply shook his head.

"Are you sure we're talking about the same person?" Her dazed look faded, replaced by one of determination. "I have a snapshot of him in my wallet. Let me get it—"

"Brenna," he said, "you saw the picture on that datasheet. Face facts. Alex got married, and you didn't know about it."

"He didn't tell me," she whispered. "How could he not— Where? When?" Brenna took a step toward him, puzzlement clouding her eyes. "Who was she? What was she like?"

He thought back to the three times he'd met Lyssa. "She was a looker," he said. "Tall and slender, with long, blond hair. Her name was Lyssa. It must have been a whirlwind courtship, because he never really mentioned dating her. One day he just showed up and announced he'd gotten married. We were best friends, and he never even brought her over to my house."

Brenna swayed. He watched as she visibly took hold of her composure. "Did he—" she licked her lips "—love her?"

"I guess." Carson shrugged, watching her closely. "How long did you say it was since you last saw Alex?"

If his question surprised her, she didn't show it.

"Less than a year. Six months. Not long enough for all this—" she gestured vaguely "—to happen."

"I've been looking for him for eighteen months. He was married two years ago," he said gently. "For whatever reason, he didn't tell you."

She closed her eyes, her stunned hurt evident in the way she tightly compressed her lips.

"I don't understand," she whispered. "What on earth has happened to my brother?"

He should have felt victorious or, at the very least, a small bit of grim satisfaction. But as he watched her, one more person The Wolf had managed to hurt with his actions, he felt only aching weariness.

"Don't try to rationalize. He lied to you. Betrayed me. Alex has changed."

"I'll say." Straightening, she gave him a dark look full of blame as she stalked to the bathroom. "And I mean to find out why."

With that parting remark, she closed the door firmly. The knob rattled enough to let him know she'd locked it. He didn't care. The bathroom had no window. If she wanted to blame him, he would let her. Brenna seemed like an intelligent woman. She would realize soon enough that he'd had nothing to do with her brother's choices.

His cell phone rang. Jack. He wanted a face-to-face and named a restaurant in town.

After one more look out the blinds—still nothing— Carson let the curtain fall back. With a tired sigh, he dropped into the room's one chair, a burnt-orange monstrosity. He pulled off his alligator boots, setting them neatly side by side under the table.

Just when he'd thought he knew everything, the situation had grown even weirder. Brenna's shock had been genuine. She truly didn't know her brother had gotten married. What reason could Alex have had for keeping his marriage a secret? Carson had doubted the marriage from the moment he'd heard about it. He found it even stranger now, since Alex hadn't even told his own sister.

When Lyssa had run off barely a month after the wedding, his partner had seemed devastated. But Alex had managed to pull himself together. Undercover, a distracted man made deadly mistakes.

In an operation the scope of the one that they'd been part of, neither of them had wanted to jeopardize things. The DEA had been after Hades' Claws for years. They'd been too close to blow it.

A remembered wave of pain swamped Carson. He ran a hand across his mouth. Once he'd thought his job defined his existence. He'd found out otherwise after his cover had been blown and his family brutally murdered. His job had meant nothing to him then. Nor did it mean anything to him now. Nothing but a vehicle for self-recrimination and blame.

The bathroom door opened. Brenna had run a damp comb through her hair and washed her face. She looked achingly young, though fierce determination shone from her eyes.

"Do you know how to get in touch with this woman?" She made a face. "Alex's wife?"

He let her have a moment to cross the room, waiting until she sat perched on the end of one bed.

"No one does, and that's saying a lot," he said. "Despite hundreds of government resources at my disposal, I couldn't find her. Though I can't say for certain, I think she might be dead."

Chapter 7

Brenna didn't believe him, not at first. Twisting her hands in her lap, she stared at Carson. Hard. With all the anger and defiance building inside her. She gave him the kind of predatory stare that made most humans back away.

But he seemed oblivious. Either that, or he simply didn't care.

"Dead," she repeated, when she could find her voice. "How convenient. Are you… Are you *sure?*"

He shrugged. She wasn't fooled by his nonchalance. Pain carved lines in his face. "Alex thought she might be. He worried."

"Was there a—" again she struggled to find the words "—a funeral?"

"No. We never found a body."

Her stomach roiled. "This is ridiculous."

"Yep." Unsmiling, he watched her. "She disappeared off the face of the earth."

Again hurt blossomed in her, bringing unwanted tears to her eyes and a need to strike out at something—anything. With an effort she stayed seated, for though she wanted to attack Carson, none of this was his fault. She took several deep breaths and was able to push her feelings aside.

"Seems I'm the bearer of bad news," he said.

"I was just thinking that," she said, startled at the way his words mirrored her thoughts. "I can't help but think—"

"That Alex's bad luck began when he met me?" His voice sounded harsh; his expression was even more so. She recognized the anger in his tone, mixed with guilt and hurt.

She jumped to her feet, jumbled emotion propelling her as she padded across the room to stand in front of him. Impassive, he regarded her, expectation plain in his face. His emotions fed her own. She couldn't tear her gaze away. They breathed in unison. Intensity flared from him to her and back again.

Brenna unclenched her fists, her heart pounding. Her anger leached out of her, becoming something else. Something that vibrated between them, silent but equally powerful.

"There's no sense in this," she said quietly, her body thrumming with desire. Though she wanted to, she seemed unable to look away. Despite his closed expression, she sensed a certain vulnerability in him.

Before, he had kissed her. Now *she* wanted to kiss *him.* She took a step closer. Then another. Reaching out, she buried her hand in his thick, sable hair.

A shudder ran through him. She felt its echo in her own thundering heartbeat. Inhaling, she took in his scent. Spicy, musky, male.

One more small movement and they met, chest to chest. She wanted more, wanted to strip off her clothes and his, then wrap herself fully around him, belly to belly. She felt him quicken against her in a rush of hardness, felt her own body respond with warmth and moisture. Flicking her tongue against the corded muscles of his neck, she tasted the salty desire on his skin, breathed it in the air.

He groaned. ''Brenna, no—''

Standing on tiptoe, she covered his mouth with her own. ''Shh.'' Urgency and need, confusion and sorrow all combined in her kiss. Her body heat increased, as it always did when she became aroused. Making wordless sounds of desire, she drank of him deeply, drawing out of him the bottled emotions he'd kept to himself for so long.

Again he groaned. Nestled snugly in the juncture of his thighs, she felt his body surge against her, even as he used his arms to push her away.

''No.'' Shoulders heaving, he turned his back to her, visibly struggling to regain control. ''Damn it, I want to forget, too, Brenna. Believe me, I do. But not this way, not by using you.''

Stung, she said the first thing that came to her mind. ''It's not a betrayal, you know.''

He swung around so quickly that she sucked in her breath.

''Every breath I take is a betrayal,'' he ground out. ''*I* should be dead, not them. And though there is a certain kind of irony in me screwing their murderer's sister, I can't do that to their memory.''

All that had burned inside her went still at his words. ''It's been eighteen months,'' she said quietly. Her throat ached. The pulse pounding in her temple, the conflicting emotions that flooded her made her head hurt. How could she want to attack and comfort someone all at the same time? How could mere words cause so much pain?

Face grim, he held up an unsteady hand. "Enough. You've had a lot of surprises today. I understand what you're feeling. You want a channel for your anger. That's understandable."

His clinical observations amused her. "And what of your own body? You wanted me, Carson. Lie to yourself all you want, but you can't hide your arousal."

"You're a beautiful woman," he said quietly. "And it's been a long time since I—"

"Made love?"

"Had sex. Think about it, Brenna. You'll realize this isn't what you want."

Though his clearheaded logic irked her, she considered his words. He'd made it clear that this would have been sex, sheer lust. Her breasts still tingled. She crossed her arms to cover her pebbled nipples and inhaled. Why had she thought that when the two of them came together, it would have been making love? Carson was right. Damn it. Though he aroused her, she didn't want a fleeting sexual fling. Much like the wolves they became when they changed, her kind mated for life.

"We need to eat," she said, changing the subject. "I'm starving."

Slowly he nodded, still watching her. "Right. We do." Glancing at the window, he frowned and consulted his watch. "Let's wait until after dark."

That made no sense. "I thought you wanted to be seen with me."

"No need." He shrugged. "Alex knows you're with me."

"You have an answer for everything, don't you?"

He dropped into the chair and he pulled on his boots. "In my line of work, you have to."

She looked at his feet. "What's with the cowboy boots?"

Running one hand lovingly over the ridged leather, he sighed. "They were a Christmas gift from my wife. I sold the house, the furniture, everything. They're all I have left of her."

Again she felt his sadness. "You must have loved her very much."

Though Carson didn't answer, he didn't have to. Brenna found herself wondering what it would be like to be loved like that.

She changed the subject. "What about the midnight deadline?"

"What about it?"

"Do you think Alex will do anything?"

His quick flash of a smile reminded her inexplicably of her brother. "I hope so."

"Sorry to disappoint you, but I don't think he will. Not with me here."

Jaw clenched, he raked his hand through his hair, reminding her of how surprisingly thick and silky it had felt when she'd touched it. Her mouth went dry. Swallowing hard, she lifted her chin.

"Do you think we need to change motels?"

He frowned. "No. Whoever threw the brick said to meet him here. As long as we watch our backs, we should be safe."

She noticed he no longer seemed to believe Alex

had written the message on the brick. "So you don't think it's a trap?"

"If it is, I'm ready." Though he sounded perfectly reasonable, she detected a hint of savage anger behind his voice.

He stood, pulling on his DEA jacket from force of habit; then, apparently having second thoughts, he yanked it off and tossed it on the bed.

"No sense in being more of a target than I have to be," he said.

She smiled. "I agree."

His expression remained deadly serious. "Brenna, I'm not joking about the danger. These people mean business. If this is a trap, we've got to be exceptionally careful. If we're lucky, we might be able to grab one of their guys and use him for leverage."

"That's your strategy?"

"I haven't come up with much of a plan yet, other than meeting with Alex."

Brenna reached for her coat. "It's just about dark," she said. "Let's go eat. We'll bring something back for Phelan."

At the sound of his name, the puppy came running. He jumped first on Carson, then, when Carson ignored him, ran to Brenna. Lavishing kisses on Phelan's small head, Brenna shook her head at Carson.

"He likes you, you know."

"Whatever." His surly tone revealed his thoughts on that subject. "What do you want to eat?"

"I don't care," she said. "As long as it's red meat."

He raised a brow. "Red meat?"

She nodded, still scratching Phelan's neck.

Just as he picked up his jacket, they heard the

sound of tires squealing, then the sickening crunch of metal hitting metal.

"Wait here," Carson ordered.

Hand already on the knob, Brenna yanked open the door first. "Like hell I will."

They rushed outside shoulder to shoulder, just in time to see the brake lights of a battered El Camino exit the parking lot and speed away.

Carson kicked at a rock with the toe of his boot. "My Tahoe."

Together, they walked toward the vehicle. The entire passenger side was crumpled. That, in addition to the shattered back windshield, made the vehicle look ready for a junkyard.

"You'd better call a tow truck," Brenna said, speaking her thoughts out loud.

Running his hand over the black metal, Carson shook his head. "It's drivable." His tone left no room for argument. "Not pretty, but I bet it'll still run."

The door to the room next to theirs opened, and a man with a shock of curly red hair peered out. After a quick look, he ducked back inside and closed the door behind him with a firm thunk.

"Carson?" One minute he'd been standing beside her, the next he'd disappeared on the other side of the Tahoe.

"He's gone," she said. "Didn't even seem curious."

Carson came around the front of the vehicle. "He's a federal agent. He doesn't want to get involved."

Hands on her hips, Brenna glared at him. She didn't need to ask how he knew. "A federal agent? So that's why you didn't want to be seen. Why didn't you tell me?"

He lifted a brow. "No reason."

His churlish growl didn't faze her. "Are they here because of the biker meeting your informant mentioned?"

"Probably. I don't know. I'm out of the loop. I'm on medical leave." He crossed to the undamaged driver's side. He held the door open for her. "Come on."

She went around and climbed up in front of him. He didn't offer to assist her, for which she was oddly grateful. She wasn't quite sure how she would feel about having his hands on her body so soon after that scorching kiss. Clambering over the console felt ungraceful, but she made short work of it, settling in her seat with an oomph.

He got in and started the engine, put the transmission in Reverse and backed from their parking spot. Other than a few rattles, clunks and clangs, the Tahoe appeared to be in sound mechanical condition.

Carson, on the other hand, appeared about as talkative as a rock.

"Do you think this was an accident?"

Carson didn't even look at her. "Get real."

"Another warning?"

"Maybe."

As they drove down Main Street in search of an open restaurant, Brenna decided to ask the question that had been nagging at her ever since she'd found that crumpled paper in his glove box. "Why are you on medical leave, anyway?"

His hands clenched on the wheel.

"Hey." She kept her voice soft. "You owe me at least that much."

A brief shadow came and went on his face. "Why? Afraid you might be traveling with a crazy person?"

She watched him, waiting.

"Fine. You want to know? They said I was losing it." Though his tone was fierce, Brenna detected bewildered hurt underneath. He made a sound of disgust. "They felt I was too intense, too focused on this investigation. That I was in danger of turning into some kind of vigilante." He shot her a grim smile. "And you know what? They were right."

From the jumble of her conflicting emotions, Brenna searched for a response. Finding none, she contented herself with watching out the window.

On the outskirts of town, a neon sign indicated that Jean's Coffee Shop was open. They turned into the parking lot.

"Vigilante," she repeated, rolling the word around in her mouth, trying to get a sense of it. "Because you want to find the man who killed your family?"

If he noticed she didn't say Alex, he gave no sign.

"Yep." Again the grim smile. "Imagine that."

"You know, I think the killer wants you here."

Carson gave her a startled look. "Why do you say that?"

"If you were a killer, wouldn't you want to finish the job?" She waited for him to make the connection.

Which he did. "But Alex wants me gone."

She wished she could ring a bell. Instead she settled for a small smile. "Bingo."

"Ergo Alex can't be the killer?" His face had gone grim again, his eyes dark and hard.

"Right." She nodded, refusing to let his obvious disbelief deflate her.

"Or maybe he regrets what he did."

Trust Carson to come up with his own kind of logic.

"You're wrong. I have a strong feeling about this. I get those sometimes."

With a savage flick of his wrist, he killed the engine. "Woman's intuition?" His tone made the words sound like a curse.

Determined to keep her smile from slipping, she nodded. "Sort of. More like animal instinct."

"Oh, yeah? Then use your sixth sense and stay alert while we grab dinner. My informant's meeting us here, and you never know who might be watching us."

Stay alert. He was right, though she doubted whoever threatened them would make a move in a public place. Still, she scanned the exterior of the small restaurant. Several cars and pickup trucks were parked outside, some snow-covered except for the windshields. The front sidewalk had been recently shoveled. Through the big front window, she could see that several others had chosen to eat their evening meal in the homey coffee shop.

"It looks okay," she told Carson.

He gave her an odd look. "If the locals eat here, the food is bound to be good."

"I meant safe."

He made a rude sound. "I don't think anywhere in this town is safe for us."

Together they walked to the door. The oddest wish struck her—she wanted to slip her hand in his. A quick glance at Carson's hard profile told her how foolish such an action would be.

A bell over the door jingled as they went inside.

"Sit anywhere." A cheerful woman with short

brown hair waved her pad at them. "I'll be with you in a minute."

Aside from a few curious glances, none of the other diners paid them any mind. Brenna studied them out of the corner of her eye. Most looked like retirees or farmers. None of them remotely resembled members of a biker gang. Nor did any appear to be government agents, though she really had no idea what a federal agent should look like.

She glanced at Carson. Openly casing the room, he hid his thoughts behind an implacable facade, no emotion showing on his masculine face. He hadn't worn a jacket, only his gray, nondescript sweatshirt, which she had to admit he filled out very well. With his broad shoulders and muscular arms, he looked dangerous, yet he moved with an easy grace that spoke of authority, determination and confidence. She wondered how he'd made it undercover, because a man like Carson would attract attention wherever he went.

They'd just settled into a booth when the waitress bustled over.

"Do you want coffee?" She set down two filled water glasses, then turned over their two cups and poured from a pot she carried with her. After sliding their steaming cups in front of them, she plunked down a couple of laminated menus and then a small pitcher of cream.

"Look these over and yell when you're ready."

Brenna glanced at the menu for steak but found only a chopped-meat version.

"The burger will be better," Carson said.

Startled, Brenna smiled. "How do you know?"

He jerked his head. "Look around."

Most of the other diners had hamburgers.

"Specialty of the house. But I'm partial to liver and onions myself."

One of her favorites. "Since there's no T-bone—" Brenna leaned forward "—I guess that'll have to do." She glanced over her shoulder. The waitress had vanished.

Looking at Carson leaning back in the booth, Brenna asked the question that had been bothering her. "Why do you suppose Alex hasn't come to talk to me himself?"

Disbelief shone in his eyes. "Come on. First off, I'm with you. He knows I want him. Then there're the Feds. Mix in bikers and drugs. It's too dangerous for him to show his face."

She sat back. "Alex knows I can take care of myself."

"You seem to have lived a pretty sheltered life." His expression doubtful, Carson took a long drink of water.

"Don't equate sheltered with weak," she warned. "I might be a librarian, but I work out four times a week. And as I said, I have a brown belt in jujitsu."

"Brown?" His lips twitched. "Why not black?"

"I'm working toward that. Give me another year," she said. Then, because she knew unless he saw her in action he would never believe her anyway, she changed the subject. "Explain what you said about not being able to find Lyssa. How can that be possible?"

"I don't know. I used every resource I had, even the FBI database. She'd vanished. Worse, I couldn't find any trace of her. I didn't have fingerprints to run.

She must have used a fake name or something. It was like she'd never existed.''

Dead? Or had someone erased her records?

Disturbed, Brenna mulled over the possibility. She would ask Alex about it when she saw him. That and numerous other things.

''She was mixed up in it somehow,'' Carson continued. ''Though I haven't been able to figure out exactly how.''

''Was she a member of Hades' Claws?''

''Are you folks ready to order?'' Smiling expectantly, the waitress appeared at their table. They both ordered the liver and onions. The waitress wrinkled her nose but wrote the order dutifully on her pad.

Taking another drink of water, Brenna waited until she was out of earshot before continuing. ''Do you think this Lyssa set my brother up?''

''How?''

Disappointed, Brenna crossed her arms. ''I don't know. You're the DEA guy. You tell me.''

Carson shook his head, making a quick, cutting motion with his hand. A young man dressed in a heavy down parka and knit cap slid in beside him. His long, dirty-blond hair hung loose around his shoulders.

''Hey.'' He cut his gaze toward Brenna. ''You must be the girlfriend. Carson told me you'd be with him tonight.''

She stiffened. Carson held up his finger, warning her silently to keep quiet.

''I got a message for you, man.'' Turning back toward Carson, the man watched with an expectant look on his bony face. ''Along with some info. Freakin' great stuff.''

Carson fished in his pocket, removing a crinkled bill and passing it over. "This better be good, Jack," he warned. "We've already gotten a couple of conflicting messages today."

So this was the informant. Carefully keeping her expression bland, Brenna pretended to be intensely interested in the chipped Formica tabletop.

"Busy day, huh?" Jack smiled, showing crooked teeth as he stuffed the money in his pocket. He let his gaze travel slowly over Brenna, making her skin crawl. "Hope everyone is all right. You don't wanna mess with some of these people. Specially the dude sending those messages."

Did he know who that was? Brenna lifted her gaze from the table. Tempted to stare him down, to intimidate him into telling her if he'd seen Alex, she leaned forward.

"Cut the crap." Impatience sounded in Carson's tone. "If you have something for me, let me have it."

With another lecherous look at Brenna, Jack leaned over and whispered in Carson's ear. Despite her excellent hearing, Brenna could not make out the words.

The waitress, carrying a heavy tray, headed for their table. Jack pushed himself up.

"Wait." Carson grabbed his arm. "Here." He pushed another crumpled bill into the other man's hand. "Buy yourself something to eat."

Jack smiled. "Thanks, man." Head down, he strode toward the door without a backward glance.

"Well?" Brenna asked, unable to contain her curiosity another second. "What did he—"

"Here you go." Setting their meals down in front of them with a thud, their waitress also refilled their water glasses. She took an inordinately long time to do it, so much so that Brenna opened her mouth, ready to ask her to leave.

"Thank you." Carson beat her to it. With a stiff nod, the woman bustled off.

"She's not happy," Carson said. "I wonder if our visitor had something to do with that."

"Who cares? So what did Jack have to say? Was his info any good?"

With a slow smile, Carson nodded. "Oh, it was good, all right. Though I suspected Alex might be here, Jack confirmed it. He told me how to find your brother."

"What?" Food forgotten, she bounded to her feet. Her stress brought on the need to change. Fighting that, she practically snarled her next words. "Come on, what are you waiting for? Let's go."

With his mouth full, he jerked his thumb in the direction of her seat. Chewing, then swallowing, he shook his head. "Calm down and don't get crazy. Eat first. You need your strength."

"What?"

"We're not going out there tonight. It's not safe. We've got to plan."

She dropped back into her chair. "I don't understand. He could be gone. he could—"

"Brenna."

She closed her mouth, trying not to inhale the tantalizing aromas of liver and fried onions.

"Eat. He's not going anywhere."

Instead of complying, she glared at him. "How do you do that?"

"How do I do what?"

"Make me feel like a little kid who's just been chastised?"

Lifting a big piece of liver to his mouth, he grinned, then ate. Chewing with gusto, he swallowed before popping some fried onions in his mouth.

"We've got to do this right. Rushing in on them in an unplanned, impulsive action could get us killed. Now eat."

Her stomach growled. He was right. Both about the need to plan and the food. She was hungry, and she needed her strength. She'd finished two-thirds of her meal before she tried again.

"So tell me—" she leaned back and blotted her mouth with the paper napkin "—why do you feel there's no hurry? How do you know Alex won't leave?"

"Though it was helpful to get confirmation, Jack didn't tell me much that I didn't already know. He gave me directions to their hideout, Nemo's place in the woods. The Hell Hole, they call it." One corner of his mouth lifted in a mocking smile. "Thursday, the date of the big meeting—that I already knew."

"If you know how to get there, let's go."

"No." His flat stare told her that he wouldn't back down. "Too dangerous. No one's going anywhere, at least not tonight. After we eat, there's another place I want to check out—a bar where they all hang."

"Do you think Alex will be there?"

He shrugged. "Who knows? It won't hurt to check it out, and any public place will be a hell of a lot safer than the hideout. If Alex isn't there, I want someone to tell him *I* am. And you." He tacked on the last as an afterthought.

Brenna sighed. "You know, planning *is* all well and good." Fighting back the need-to-change-fueled energy, she clenched the edge of the table and leaned forward. "But we can make a plan in a few minutes. Why don't we go out to the Hell Hole now, instead of this bar? I don't understand why we can't simply show up and force a meeting."

"You *are* crazy," he said, no humor in his deep voice. "That place is probably protected better than Fort Knox. They'd shoot you before they'd let you get within fifty feet of them."

"You don't know—"

"I don't want to be such an easy target." He spread his hands on the table. "With such an important drug buy about to happen, tension is pretty high. Anything could set off violence. Their old enemy showing up on their doorstep would rank pretty high on their list of triggers."

She sighed. He was right, but she had one advantage that he didn't know about. She could change.

"Then let me go alone. They don't know me. They have no reason to mistrust me."

"You don't know what kind of people you're dealing with."

"No." She swallowed. "Nor do I much care. All I want is to talk to my brother."

"Even if doing so could endanger his life?"

Chapter 8

That stopped her cold. "What do you mean?"

"If Alex is still undercover and you reveal you're his sister, what happens then, with his cover blown? Do you want to give them ammunition to use against him?"

She hadn't thought of that. "Do you think he is? Still undercover?"

"Of course." But the bitter twist of Carson's mouth told her he didn't really believe it. "Anything's possible."

She sighed. "I want to help Alex, not hurt him."

"Then we stick with my original plan. We need to bring him to us, not the other way around. That allows him to choose the time and the place when things are safest for him."

She nodded reluctantly. What he said made sense, damn it. If she were a mere human woman. While he had a point—no sense in endangering her brother—

Carson had no idea what she could do. If she could get close enough to the Hell Hole, she could signal her brother. He could change and meet her in the forest. As wolves, they would blend into the shadows. No one would see; no one would know.

Decision made, she took another bite of the tasty liver. She would pretend to agree with Carson's plan, wait until he slept, then sneak out under the cover of darkness. Alone.

Glancing up to find Carson watching her, she forced a smile. "Did your informant—Jack—tell you anything else?"

"No." He polished off a few more of the greasy onions. "Same old stuff."

"Then why'd you pay him? If his information wasn't useful, couldn't you get your money back?"

He laughed. "There are no 'satisfaction guaranteed' deals in this kind of thing. And he's my link with Hades' Claws, because he knows a couple of them. I want to keep him talking."

Confused, she shrugged. "I don't see what else he could possibly tell you."

"You'd be surprised. Sometimes the most interesting information comes out when you think there's nothing left to learn. Excuse me." Signaling the waitress, he smiled pleasantly. "I'd like a to-go box, please. And the check."

At Brenna's questioning look, he pointed to her plate. "For Phelan," he said. "I saved some, too."

So he had. Between his leftovers and hers, the puppy should have enough to eat. Still, it was surprising—and touching—that Carson had cared enough to remember. He'd seemed so determined to keep even the affectionate dog at a distance. She still planned to pick up a bag of bona fide puppy food later, but decided to keep that fact to herself for now.

After he paid the check, they headed into the now-dark night. The parking lot wasn't well lit, and Carson winced when they rounded the corner and he saw his battered, black Tahoe.

"What a beater," he said, shaking his head. "That SUV is only three years old. It was in such great shape before all this."

Staring at his vehicle, Brenna couldn't manage a laugh. With every minute, every hour, her sense of urgency increased. She needed to talk to Alex. Not tomorrow, not in a few days, but *now*.

But how would she ever find the compound if Carson didn't show her the location? She decided to make one more attempt to convince him of the need to act immediately.

"No one will know if we drive out to the compound. I just want to see where it is. It's dark, and we don't have to stop."

He didn't even look at her. "Tomorrow," he said.

Fine. She'd tried. Now she had to figure out a way to make him tell her what he knew. Once she had the location of the hideout, she would wait until Carson was asleep and go out there herself. This would give her a much-needed opportunity to change, as well— a wolf could lope through the forest much faster than a human.

Phelan smelled the leftover liver the second they walked in the door. Wagging his tail, he began to drool. Brenna emptied the pungent bag on the bathroom floor, letting the eager puppy gobble his fill.

"Hey." Carson put his hand on her shoulder. "Don't worry so much. We'll drive out to the Hell

Hole tomorrow, in broad daylight. Hiding nothing. Though we won't—'' he shot her a warning look ''—go in. I want Alex to feel sufficiently threatened so he'll arrange a private meeting, but not enough to make some crazy person start taking potshots at us.''

''Broad daylight?'' She echoed his words. ''Since they're trying to kill you, do you think that's wise?''

Letting his hand fall, he shrugged. ''We need to check the place out thoroughly. We can't if it's dark. We'll just have to be careful.''

Brenna nodded. ''I hope you're right,'' she murmured. ''How far away is this place?''

''About five miles north.''

Five miles. A long way for a human to walk. Not so far for a long-limbed wolf. Still, she needed more specific directions. She couldn't go wandering around town after she'd changed.

''How far are we from the Vermont border?''

This time her question earned a hard look. ''Why do you want to know? Planning on seeing if you can make it to Canada?''

Though the Canadian wilderness was home to many of the Pack, fleeing had never entered her mind. ''Not without Alex.''

They stared at each other for a moment, neither speaking. She felt like a lone wolf unexpectedly meeting a larger wolf in the forest. Finally Carson looked away, a muscle working in his cheek.

''How long will it take you to get ready?''

Perplexed, she looked at him.

''To go check out the bar.'' He glanced at his watch, silver gleaming against his tanned skin. ''It's nine-thirty.''

The biker bar. She'd forgotten about that. With a

sigh, she smoothed her hands over the front of her faded jeans. "I'm ready now. I don't have any other clothes. Besides, jeans and boots seem to fit in well in bars."

"Where's your vest?"

"Vest?"

"The black leather one you wore in the bar where you met me." With a wicked smile that came and went too quickly, he crossed to the door. "It looks good on you. If you can find it, put it on."

Was that a teasing note in his voice? Had pigs learned to fly?

"Was that a compliment?"

He shrugged.

After locating the vest where she'd tossed it on a chair, she slipped it over her arms. "I need to let Phelan out first."

"I'll do it." The quickness of his gruff response brought an involuntary smile to her face.

"He'd like that," she said.

"I'm only taking him so you'll stay in here." With a grimace, he looked at Phelan. "Come here."

The puppy didn't move. Cocking his head, he looked up at Brenna, then at Carson.

"He's confused. You sound too angry."

"I'm not." Carson snapped his fingers and whistled. "Let's go." He reached for the door. "Outside."

Starting forward, again Phelan hesitated, studying Carson with his head cocked.

"Go," Brenna ordered softly. "Be a good dog."

Tail held high, the puppy trotted over to Carson, sitting at his feet and gazing up at him.

"How old do you think he is?" Carson regarded both Brenna and Phelan with a frown.

She shrugged. "I don't know. Pretty young, I'd guess. Close to a year maybe."

He shook his head. "You stay inside." Opening the door, he stepped out, Phelan trotting at his heels.

For about ten seconds she resisted the urge to peek out the window at them. Then she gave in and looked. When she did, she watched Phelan romping in the shadowy field next to the parking lot. He found a stick and ran to Carson. Carson hesitated. Phelan jumped, stick still between his teeth, and pawed at Carson's jeans. Finally Carson crouched low, ruffled the puppy's fur and then tossed the piece of wood. The two played this game for a few moments before they started back toward the room.

Hurriedly, she let the curtain fall. With a peculiar ache in her chest, she went into the bathroom to study herself in the small mirror.

"Not good, Bren," she muttered. With her hair curling around her shoulders in an untamed riot, she looked like a wild woman. Biker mama, hoochie-coochie. Not at all like the prim-and-proper librarian the people of her hometown knew. Even her own brother might not recognize her, with her tight jeans and leather vest. With a touch of bright-colored lipstick she could easily pass for a biker groupie, hunting in a biker bar for a man to take home for the night.

She looked, she thought with a sigh, exactly as she needed to look. But part of her wondered if the vixen she saw in the mirror was the way Carson saw her.

Though she didn't like Carson's plan, she was glad he'd decided to go to the bar. Action was always better than inaction, as far as she was concerned. She didn't have much patience for waiting. Unless she was on a hunt, which meant perpetual motion, no matter how stealthy and slow, she felt restless and unfocused. Which also might help explain her unwarranted fascination with Carson himself.

The front door opened, and Phelan bounded inside.

"Ready?" Carson glanced at her. A slow smile spread over his rugged face. "I'll be damned."

"What?"

"You look…different." He cocked his head. "Not sure how you did it. Maybe it's the hair."

She lifted her chin. "Or the vest. Do you think I look biker-mama enough?"

His smile faded. The appreciative glow in his dark eyes vanished. His bleak, determined expression returned.

"Yep." He sounded gruff, cold. The original Carson was back.

Slowly she studied him, hating the ache behind her throat, the tightness in her chest. She'd always had a compulsion to heal wounded creatures. She had to remember he wasn't an animal—not like her. He hadn't asked her to heal him, wouldn't even welcome her interference in the tight-fisted grip he had on his own suffering.

"Let's go." As he reached for the doorknob, they both heard the door from the next room squeak open.

Carson froze, then held up his hand. Silent, they listened.

Speaking in low voices, several men walked outside.

Brenna could only make out a few words, including Hades' Claws. With her overdeveloped sense of smell, she detected that they all wore too much aftershave, a spicy scent often worn by teenage boys.

"Damn," Carson swore in a whisper. "What the hell are they doing?"

She wrinkled her nose in a grimace. "Do you think they're getting ready to raid the Hell Hole?"

He swore again. Tension radiated from him. "I hope not. That'd be stupid. They must be FBI—they sure as hell can't be DEA."

"Why not?"

"Because the drug deal isn't until Thursday. Unless it's been changed, which I doubt. I would have heard about it if it had. They'd have to wait until then if they wanted to collect the evidence and all the players."

The men outside continued to argue, their voices low. She heard footsteps—a single man walking away, not the entire group. A car door slammed; an engine cranked. Still the small group stayed outside the door, continuing their discussion more quietly, even as the car sputtered off. Finally they went back inside, slamming the door behind them so hard the walls shook.

"Gotta be FBI," Carson repeated. His teeth gleamed white in the darkness. "At least if *they* see me, they won't recognize me."

He stayed put, his wide-legged stance still blocking the way out.

Brenna didn't move, either. "What just happened?"

Lifting one shoulder in a shrug, he snorted. "Who knows? Maybe one guy went out for pizza."

Or maybe that one guy had gone to case the Hell Hole under the cover of night. Like she still planned to do.

Carson's cell phone rang. Exchanging a glance

with Brenna, he answered. The conversation was brief and monosyllabic, at least on Carson's end.

"Yes. No, sir. I won't. In the city. Yes, sir. That's great. Yes."

As he snapped the phone closed, he grimaced. "My boss. Says someone called him, thought they saw me. He wanted to make sure I was nowhere near here."

"Where'd you tell him you were?"

"New York City."

"Do you think he believed you?"

"I don't know." He rubbed the back of his neck. "He's given instructions to the guys on the team—if they see me, they're to arrest me, no questions asked."

"That's not good." She sat down on the edge of the bed and yawned. "Does your neck hurt?"

"Tension."

Exhaustion washed through her. The near-violent urge to change that had assaulted her in the coffee shop had passed for now, leaving fatigue in its place. She needed to rest before attempting to sneak out later. Turning her head, she glanced at the bedside clock, numerals glowing red. Ten o'clock.

"Maybe going to the bar right now isn't a good idea. I'm tired, and you look worn-out, too. Let's get some sleep." She spoke before he could, muffling another yawn with her hand.

"I'm not hiding. There's just one more group of people we have to watch out for, that's all. Let's go." His gaze bore into hers. His sharp tone indicated he thought she'd lost her mind.

She suppressed a smile. "Leaving right now is a bad idea, with those guys so close. We can check out the bar tomorrow, after we go to the Hell Hole."

An Important Message from the Editors

Dear Reader,

Because you've chosen to read one of our fine romance novels, we'd like to say "thank you!" And, as a special way to thank you, we've selected two more of the books you love so well, plus an exciting Mystery Gift, to send you absolutely FREE!

Please enjoy them with our compliments...

Pam Powers

Peel off Seal and Place Inside...

EDITOR'S FREE GIFT SEAL THANK YOU

How to validate your Editor's
FREE GIFT
"Thank You"

1. Peel off gift seal from front cover. Place it in space provided at right. This automatically entitles you to receive 2 FREE BOOKS and a fabulous mystery gift.

2. Send back this card and you'll get 2 brand-new Silhouette Intimate Moments® novels. These books have a cover price of $4.75 each in the U.S. and $5.75 each in Canada, but they are yours to keep absolutely free.

3. There's no catch. You're under no obligation to buy anything. We charge nothing—ZERO—for your first shipment. And you don't have to make any minimum number of purchases—not even one!

4. The fact is, thousands of readers enjoy receiving their books by mail from the Silhouette Reader Service™. They enjoy the convenience of home delivery...they like getting the best new novels at discount prices BEFORE they're available in stores...and they love their *Heart to Heart* subscriber newsletter featuring author news, horoscopes, recipes, book reviews and much more!

5. We hope that after receiving your free books you'll want to remain a subscriber. But the choice is yours— to continue or cancel, any time at all! So why not take us up on our invitation, with no risk of any kind. You'll be glad you did!

6. Remember...just for validating your Editor's Free Gift Offer, we'll send you THREE gifts, *ABSOLUTELY FREE!*

GET A *Free* MYSTERY GIFT...

SURPRISE MYSTERY GIFT COULD BE YOURS _FREE_ AS A SPECIAL "THANK YOU" FROM THE EDITORS OF SILHOUETTE

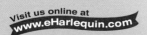

Visit us online at
www.eHarlequin.com

The Editor's "Thank You" Free Gifts Include:

- Two BRAND-NEW romance novels!
- An exciting mystery gift!

PLACE FREE GIFT SEAL HERE

Yes I have placed my Editor's "Thank You" seal in the space provided above. Please send me 2 free books and a fabulous Mystery Gift. I understand I am under no obligation to purchase any books, as explained on the back and on the opposite page.

345 SDL DZ6R   **245 SDL DZ66**

FIRST NAME	LAST NAME

ADDRESS

APT.#   CITY

STATE/PROV.   ZIP/POSTAL CODE   (S-IM-06/04)

Thank You!

The Silhouette Reader Service™ — Here's how it works:

Accepting your 2 free books and gift places you under no obligation to buy anything. You may keep the books and gift and return the shipping statement marked "cancel." If you do not cancel, about a month later we'll send you 6 additional books and bill you just $3.99 each in the U.S., or $4.74 each in Canada, plus 25¢ shipping & handling per book and applicable taxes if any.* That's the complete price and — compared to cover prices of $4.75 each in the U.S. and $5.75 each in Canada — it's quite a bargain! You may cancel at any time, but if you choose to continue, every month we'll send you 6 more books, which you may either purchase at the discount price or return to us and cancel your subscription.

*Terms and prices subject to change without notice. Sales tax applicable in N.Y. Canadian residents will be charged applicable provincial taxes and GST.

If offer card is missing write to: The Silhouette Reader Service, 3010 Walden Ave., P.O. Box 1867, Buffalo, NY 14240-1867

BUSINESS REPLY MAIL
FIRST-CLASS MAIL   PERMIT NO. 717-003   BUFFALO, NY

POSTAGE WILL BE PAID BY ADDRESSEE

SILHOUETTE READER SERVICE
3010 WALDEN AVE
PO BOX 1867
BUFFALO NY 14240-9952

NO POSTAGE
NECESSARY
IF MAILED
IN THE
UNITED STATES

He stayed where he was, though he made sure the door was closed, sliding the dead bolt into place. "I don't like this," he muttered.

"But you said they're FBI and won't recognize you, so why are you so worried? Or do you think there's some kind of bulletin out on you, too?"

"Bulletin?"

"You know—" she kept her voice casual "—like the fake one you showed me on Alex."

As she'd expected, he answered instantly. "It wasn't fake." Frustration showed in his clipped tone. "What is it going to take to convince you?"

Hands on her hips, she faced him. "How easy would it be to forge one of those things?"

He crossed his arms. "Give me a break."

"I want to know."

"Why would anyone want to forge an FBI datasheet?"

This time she waited for the implication to sink in.

When it did, Carson only shook his head. "The datasheet was real. Don't lie to yourself," he said gently. "It'll only hurt more in the end if you do."

Her heart sank. "I'm going to bed."

"Suit yourself." Though he sounded as though he still intended to hit the bar, he made no move to leave. He watched her while she prepared her bed, pulling down the discolored bedspread and brushing off the sheets. She padded over to the bathroom, chin held high and closed the door.

After she emerged, Carson sat on the edge of the bed opposite hers, head down, hand pressed against his temples. He'd pulled off his boots and placed them neatly underneath the table by the window.

"Look, I—"

"This is not a game," he said, interrupting her. "You need to understand that. You could be killed."

"So could you."

"Yeah, I could." He lifted his head to look at her and the bleakness in his dark eyes nearly made her cry out. "But the difference is, I don't care."

"*I* care." The words slipped out, words she'd had no intention of saying—ever. Mortified, she swallowed hard.

"Don't." His one-word response said it all. She should have thanked him for reminding her of the chasm between them. He didn't want or need her pity *or* her friendship. She ought to be grateful that she couldn't give him love.

Love? Was she so foolish as to let herself care for such a wounded man? And a human, at that. Horrified, Brenna thought of her former fiancé, Jeff, and his reaction when he learned she could change. Finding out about her had cost Jeff his life.

She climbed into bed, hating the heat she felt in her cheeks. She'd nearly hung herself out to dry, telling him she actually cared.

Meanwhile Carson's one-word warning hung in the stuffy air between them.

She closed her eyes. She couldn't think straight, not with the ever-present desire to change simmering faster in her blood again. If she got a brief nap, she would awaken in a few hours refreshed and ready to go. To think, to decide. To change.

Carson clicked out the light, plunging the room into welcome darkness. The faint but pungent scent of their dinner hung in the air.

"I can't protect you, you know," he said finally, his acrid certainty final.

"Protect me?" She sat up. "How many times do I have to tell you? I can take care of myself."

He made a sound, the strangled sound of a wild animal in pain. She nearly went to him. Only by holding on to his warning was she able to keep herself immobile.

"Get some sleep." She rolled onto her side in an attempt to do the same. The room felt unbearably hot, and finally she struggled out of her jeans and sweatshirt, covering herself with only the sheet.

An hour later, still awake, she gave up. Since counting sheep only made her hungry, she tried not to listen to Carson's restless tossing and turning, and focused on relaxation techniques instead.

They didn't work, either. Restless and impatient, she couldn't stand it any longer. Sending Phelan a quieting thought, she rose soundlessly. Dressing in the dark was easy. She stepped into her jeans, shimmying them over her hips. Her sweatshirt came next, then her socks and shoes, and she was done. She left her parka behind. She would be warm enough once she changed. With one last look at the puppy curled up on the end of her bed, she made her way toward the door.

"Going somewhere?" Carson's scent suddenly filled her nostrils as he loomed up in front of her, blocking her with his body. His sleep-roughened voice seemed deeper, more suggestive. Startled, Brenna jumped, fighting back the instinctive urge to change.

"Outside," she said, managing not to growl. "I need some fresh air."

"Right." He didn't move. She blinked, taunted by

an insane urge to run her hands down the length of him.

Desire, or the haunting scent of need, filled the space between them.

"I'm going outside." Attempting to push past him, she felt a spark as her hand connected with his bare stomach. She jerked her hand away as if the feel of him burned her. Sometime in the night he, too, must have removed his jeans. An ache started deep within her, pulsing with her accelerated heartbeat.

"Move," she snarled, furious at her body's reaction to him. Instead, his arms came around her and crushed her against him. Her sweatshirt rode up, giving her bare skin a touch of his.

Naked except for his boxers, he was muscular and hard in more ways than one. A thrill went through her, even as she debated using her martial arts training to free herself. But, unable to resist, she gave an experimental wiggle against him, as though she were only a helpless human female, trying to free herself. Immediately his body responded. She bit back a moan as he surged against her belly.

Adrenaline, frustration, desire. The urge to change always made her other animal instincts more pronounced. And she wanted him—badly. She could still scent her own desire. Though his sense of smell couldn't be as developed as hers, Carson could surely detect her urgent need. If not from the scent of her, then from the way her nipples pebbled against him. In the darkness, she could see only his silhouette, though his heartbeat thundered under her cheek.

He broke out in a sweat, the light sheen only adding to his appeal. Unable to resist, she licked his neck lightly, the salty taste heady. He moaned, a strangled curse as he ground himself against her.

Now she wished she hadn't gotten dressed.

He captured her wrists with both hands. She saw images of him tethering her to the bed, ravishing her eager body with his mouth, before he covered her with his body and made savage love to her.

Instead he released her and pushed her gently toward her bed.

"Back to sleep."

She laughed, the sound almost a purr. "Is that an order?"

"Brenna…"

With slow, deliberate motions, she kicked off her shoes, peeled off her jeans. He swore again, still motionless in front of the door. Without hesitation she removed her bra and panties, thrilling to the feel of herself naked, desirable, powerful and aroused.

She moved silently, knowing he couldn't fully see her in the darkness. He still wanted her, she knew in an instant, as she rubbed her cheek against his chest.

"No," he said, but his body disagreed. Delighted, Brenna let herself touch him, chest and arms as well as there, and was rewarded by his groan.

She kissed his corded shoulders, then his neck, pressing her bare breasts into his chest.

One minute he was with her, the next he pushed her away and moved toward the bathroom.

"Fine," he said, disgust and anger in his voice. "You win. If you want to leave, I won't stop you. Just don't try to seduce me again." And he slammed the bathroom door, leaving her shocked and aching.

Five-thirty in the morning. Only masochists rose at this hour. Carson punched his pillow and listened again for the sound of Brenna's breathing. He'd had a torturously rough night. Fitful dozing only, hanging on to the sharp edge of awareness so he would know if she tried to climb into his bed. Asleep, he could not resist her, though even the thought of her silky limbs intertwined with his made him uncomfortably aware of his own hard and aching body. His own need and desire.

Guilt filled him. He shouldn't want her, but he did. Pushing away his erotic thoughts, he gave up his futile attempt to go back to sleep and sat up.

If he focused on what he'd come to do instead of what he wanted to do to Alex's sister, maybe his raging hormones would subside.

Today. Today they would drive out to the encampment, the last thing those murderous thugs would expect. And, since Alex seemed so intent on warning him away, Carson wanted to show him beyond a shadow of a doubt that he wouldn't let Brenna go anywhere. Not until he got answers. He found it hard to believe that a man as cold-blooded as Alex had become would worry about her at all. And if he did, surely Alex knew Carson. He wouldn't let her get hurt. Not on his watch. Two lives lost had been more than enough. He would die before he let that happen again.

Alex had offered a trade—himself for his sister. Right. Like Alex would really turn himself in on Friday, the day after all the drugs and cash were supposed to trade hands. No, Carson would bet his last dollar Alex would be on some plane to an undisclosed Caribbean country.

The rising sun leaked around the edges of the

heavy, dust-covered curtains. Padding to the window on bare feet, Carson drew back the drapes, letting the fresh light of the new morning in through the dirt-streaked glass.

Today would be a good day. He repeated the words like a mantra. Though he hadn't had a truly good day since he'd lost his family, each hour that brought him closer to achieving his goal he deemed a success.

In the bed next to him, Brenna stirred, stretching her supple, slender body like a cat. She'd kicked off her covers in the night, and the sweatshirt she wore rode up one shapely hip. He stared, unable to resist, drinking in her unconscious sensuality like whiskey and feeling it burn in much the same way.

Whiskey had been his salvation once, when every day had seemed like the darkest night. No more. He needed every sense sharp and ready to bring down his enemy. The need for such oblivion still haunted him, especially when his stomach ached and he wanted to forget.

He focused his attention away from the bed next to him.

Brenna. Damn her. When he'd woken in the night and found himself holding her, fully aroused, he'd wanted her with a savage mindlessness that stunned him. Later, after he'd rejected her, she seemed hurt. No doubt an act; yet he couldn't let go of the knowledge that she wanted him as badly as he desired her. Still.

Later again, watching her try to sleep, at times she'd seemed as if she were burning from the inside out. She'd seemed like a wild animal, predatory, fierce. Looking at her, Carson had thought for one startled second that he still lingered in some weird dream. Then she'd rolled over, stretched and become Brenna again, and he'd felt even more foolish.

Time to get back to reality.

"Hey." Reaching down, he shook her shoulder, ignoring the leap his heart gave in reaction to her soft skin. "Wake up."

She came awake instantly, moving away from him and rising with a compact movement that made him remember her claim to martial arts training. The more he came to know this woman, the more he questioned his sanity.

He shouldn't even care, didn't care, not really, but sometimes, just watching her made him remember how sweet his life had once been.

"Take the first shower." His voice sounded gruff, brisk, a drill sergeant who'd actually taken that imaginary shot of whiskey. "Make it quick. We've got a lot to do today."

After her first surprised look at his sharp tone, she narrowed her eyes. He was almost disappointed when she didn't argue, merely ducking her head in a quick nod before grabbing her duffel bag and disappearing into the bathroom.

The shower started. For a moment he entertained the enticing image of her naked, water sluicing over her creamy skin, the soapy washcloth touching her breasts. Then, muttering a curse, he forced his thoughts to the target at hand—the Internet maps he'd obtained of Nemo's isolated estate, the Hell Hole.

The shower shut off after five minutes. The bathroom door opened a moment after that.

"Your turn." She matched his earlier tone, toweling her hair with one hand. She'd donned a beige

T-shirt and a pair of olive khakis, again making him think of the military.

With a nod, he grabbed a clean pair of jeans and a shirt from his own duffel, and turned sideways to go past her into the bathroom. Though he had no doubt she'd planned to sneak off in the night, he closed the door behind him. If she wanted to go it alone, on foot, more power to her. However, no matter how badly she wanted to find Alex, he didn't believe she would do anything that stupid. And he needed space to clear his head.

But even here, he couldn't escape her. He took a deep breath and smelled...flowers. A floral, feminine scent filled the small room. He shook his head. Chest tight, he turned on the water, setting the knob to hot, and stepped inside the shower.

A few minutes later, clean and dressed, he pushed open the door and stepped into the bedroom. Empty.

Refusing to believe she'd really gone, he caught himself about to peer under the bed. A glance at the front door showed the chain had been taken off, the dead bolt unlocked.

His heart began to pound. He wanted to curse his own stupidity. He battled the urge to run outside after her, to see if she'd left tracks.

Damn! She'd left. And he'd given her the opportunity. Now she would warn her brother, and Alex would disappear, exactly as he'd disappeared eighteen months ago.

Or, worse, Hades' Claws would see her, know she was with Carson and kill or capture her. Once again he would have failed to keep an innocent safe.

He'd blown it. His careful planning—gone. All for nothing. All because, for the first time in years, he'd allowed himself to think with his body—and maybe a little bit of his heart.

Chapter 9

He would find her. Plain and simple. Holstering his gun, he grabbed his jacket just as the front door creaked open. Wearing the black DEA cap at a jaunty angle, Brenna brandished a couple of white bags in one hand, grinning.

"I brought breakfast." Her wide smile faded when she got a good look at his face. She kicked the door closed, juggling two takeout cups of coffee in her other hand.

"What is it? What's wrong?" After setting down her burden on the dresser, she crossed her arms and studied him. "Are you all right? What happened?"

"You went outside. Unprotected." His words came out in a snarl.

"I was hungry." She shrugged. "So sue me."

"Hungry?" An explosion built inside, but he tried to contain his anger, worry and, yes, relief as he strode across the room. When he reached her, he gave in, grabbing her small shoulders and yanking her into him. Holding her tight. ''What the hell were you thinking?''

She froze, completely still in his hold. Unable to help himself, he breathed in her scent, the flower-like aroma of spring. No doubt she felt the still-too-fast thumping of his heart in his chest, the lightning-swift catch of his breath as his anger shifted into desire. Unwanted desire, sudden but razor sharp just the same.

She lifted her head to look up at him, long lashes shadowing her coffee-colored eyes. Though he wanted to step away, to drop his arms and let her go, she gave a soft cry and wound herself around him. The invitation of her parted lips was more than he, no saint for sure, could even begin to resist.

As he bent his head, she lifted her mouth, and he was lost.

Lifting her arms, she twined them around his neck. Belly to belly, they kissed. She tasted of spearmint toothpaste and woman. He wanted her. Like an eager youth in a roadster, his body urged him to take her. Now. Hard and fast and deep. Impossible, without them stripping off their clothes. Would she let him inside her? The way she curled into him, sinuous and willing, told him she might.

Brenna. Heat and musk, no longer spring but the lush heat of summer. Brenna.

Think. He needed to think. Through the red haze of desire, he forced himself to use common sense. He couldn't do this—*they* couldn't do this. Cursing under his breath, he pushed her away. He would have laughed cynically at himself if he didn't hurt so damn bad.

And she—what must she think? Lately all he'd done was paw at her like some horny adolescent, then push her away. He, of all people, should know better.

Unable to look at her, his every sense on overloaded overdrive, he spun away, staggering like a drunk. One step wasn't enough, so he took two. Then three, until he stood as far away as the motel room would allow. Wiping a hand across his mouth, he took a ragged breath, exhaled, then took another.

Behind him, she made a sound. Not a whimper, not exactly, but a sound of regret, nonetheless. Even so, he refused to turn around, afraid if he did he would drown again in the frank sensuality of her gaze.

"This isn't acceptable," he said harshly, furious with himself and with her for the lure she represented. He should have been beyond such temptations.

Paper rustled. He smelled eggs and ham and croissant. That must have been what she'd brought for them to eat. His stomach, which, like the rest of his body, had taken on a mind of its own, growled.

"Breakfast," she said. If her voice sounded overly bright, he pretended not to notice. "And coffee. Hot."

While she fussed with the grease-spotted bag, he stalked to the dresser and snatched up one cup. As he pried off the lid, the steam told him it was still scalding. Good. She'd brought it black. Even better.

Moving back to the window, he peered out. He took a quick gulp, letting the coffee scald his throat.

"We need to talk," she said, sounding determined and angry and scared all at once.

"No." He took another swallow. "We don't." If, like most women, she pressed the issue, he would simply apologize and tell her it wouldn't happen again. Hell, he would make damn sure it didn't happen again. No matter what.

Even now, guilt still lay coiled in his gut. Not guilt because he'd taken unfair advantage—no, that wasn't it. Brenna, with her eager mouth and roving hands, had been more than willing. This self-directed loathing was because he shouldn't have wanted her. Shouldn't have, couldn't have but still did. Right this very moment his blood still burned with desire for her. If he was stupid enough to close his eyes, he knew he would still see her, knew he would still dream at night of the yearning on her mobile face, dream of pushing himself deep inside her. Knew he would still want her with every breath he took.

"Damn it all to hell." He had to get a grip—no, not that kind of grip. A grip on the crashing crescendo inside his chest.

"Do you want to eat?" Her voice sounded normal now, clear and unaffected. Which both angered and pleased him.

"Yeah." He forced himself to meet her eyes. Seeing nothing but pleasant concern made his gut clench.

Holding out one of the white bags, she flashed a small smile. "It's okay, Carson. Come eat."

Her cool-and-collected look almost fooled him. Almost. But her nipples still poked against the front of her faded T-shirt, and the irises of her eyes were dilated.

And he was hard again, just from one look.

"This has to stop."

"Yes," she agreed. He hadn't realized he'd actually spoken the thought out loud.

"Your food's getting cold." She tossed him the white bag.

Suddenly ravenous, he pulled out the croissant and took a huge bite. While he chewed, Brenna wadded up her bag and napkin and tossed them at the trash can. They bounced off the rim and went in.

"Two points," she muttered. Then she glanced at the nightstand clock. "Are you about ready? I want to get this show on the road."

He nearly choked on his food. Then he laughed, feeling the tension ease. "Let's go," he said.

Following her outside, he tried not to notice her sexy behind or the gentle sway of her hips. Together, they climbed into his vehicle. After clicking the seat belt in place, she folded her hands in her lap, as prim as if they were heading to church.

Once out of the parking lot, the Tahoe's rattles and creaks attested to its recent beating. Carson found a radio station that played oldies and turned the volume up louder than usual. The last thing he needed was Brenna continuing in her earlier we-need-to-talk vein.

The drive north down Main Street took less than five minutes. At the end of the town square, they took a left. On the outskirts of town, the forest took over, scraggly branches of leafless trees giving the road a stark, primitive appearance. The houses, few and far between, were set back at the ends of long, tree-lined driveways that snaked away from the road. In the summer the trees would shield these brick monstrosities from view. But right now dappled sunlight mingled with the bare branches, exposing the massive homes in a sort of primitive beauty. Even so, the limited sunlight was unsuccessful in melting the snow and ice alongside the road.

"Beautiful," Brenna said.

He glanced at her and saw she was studying the

landscape, an intense look of yearning on her face. He recognized that craving—identified with it, as well. He, too, often longed for what he'd lost—a home. But for him it was like crying over spilt milk. But Brenna had a home somewhere upstate, where she worked as a librarian. That is, if her story was true.

As they followed the curve of the road, the houses became fewer, the trees thicker, the scrubby underbrush wild.

He consulted his handwritten directions and slowed to a crawl.

"It should be right about…there." An uneven stone wall wound between the trees. Flanked by two towering cement monoliths, the wall ended at a huge, black iron gate, which guarded the long driveway that disappeared into the trees. The rock wall looped and dipped, high and low, some areas crumbling, others tall with the look of haphazard repair, as though installed by a crew of inebriated men.

It appeared to be five feet tall at the lowest point, well over eight at the highest. With its varying height and width, the wall had only one constant that Carson could see—the flat stone top was inlaid with broken glass, bright colors sparkling in the winter sun. All the shards pointed outward, sharp and deadly.

"Hell of a deterrent," he said. "I've seen a few walls like that before, but only in Mexico and Brazil."

Though she nodded at his words, Brenna continued to study the wall. Too tall for her to leap in her wolf form, impossible to climb as a human, the barricade seemed insurmountable. No doubt that had been the builder's intention, she thought with a wry smile. She would have to figure out a way around it.

"How do they open the gate?"

"By remote." Carson pointed to a small speaker box set into the stone. "You have to be admitted. And they have cameras, see?"

Not one but two cameras were aimed at the gate.

"They probably have motion sensors, too, don't they?" Her heart sank. "The place is well guarded."

"Yeah." His gaze searched her face, as if he knew what she was considering. "Of course it is. They have too much to lose to be careless."

She studied the wall again. Somewhere there had to be a spot low enough for her to jump. As a wolf, if she took a running start, she might be able to leap over. Of course, the consequences were she to fail could be deadly—or merely a scraped wolf belly. Either way, she had to try.

Just thinking about changing brought the urge so strongly that her mouth went dry. For a moment Brenna battled herself, hoping Carson wouldn't notice. It had been far too long since she'd assumed her wolf form.

"Ok, so that's it." After making a U-turn in the road, he accelerated back toward town. "We can't drive in there unannounced. And with the cameras aimed at the gate, they'd spot us. We're just checking the place out. I don't want them to know I was here."

"We," she corrected automatically. "We were here." She craned her neck for one last look, marking the stately oaks that guarded the gated drive. Though a good distance from the motel, the Hell Hole was not too far for her to run in a single night. To lope there and back would certainly be exhausting, but such a distance was well within her capabilities once she'd changed. Breaching the wall would be her main problem.

He broke into her chain of thought. "What are you thinking?"

Suddenly aware of his scrutiny, she turned in her seat and said the first thing that came to mind. "This bar you want to check out, do you think it will be safe?"

He shrugged, watching her from the corner of his eye. "No place is safe for us. Especially if they know we've been out here, casing their hideout. If you're worried, you can wait in here."

"Right." She drew the word out in a sarcastic drawl. "Since they're shooting at you, why don't *you* wait in here and let me check out the bar?"

To her surprise he laughed. Not the cynical, no-humor sound he'd been prone to since she'd met him, but a deep peal of belly laughter that made her smile in return.

"You didn't dress in your biker-babe outfit," he reminded her. Amazed at the way humor lit up his craggy face, she was so busy staring that she nearly didn't respond.

"Didn't feel like it," she said. Noting again the sharp tug of sexual awareness, she tore her gaze away from him.

"With you wearing that DEA jacket—" she touched the brim of her cap "—and me in this DEA hat, we don't need to look like bikers anymore, do we?

He laughed again. "No. Now we look like targets." Still chuckling, he reached over and took the hat from her head. "I think we'll leave the DEA gear in the Tahoe."

Bringing one hand up to comb through her flattened hair, she smiled back. "Ok. Now let me in on the joke?"

He shook his head, the grin fading, though traces of humor still sparkled in his eyes. "I just had this mental image of you in a packed biker bar, doing a *Crouching Tiger, Hidden Dragon* routine and taking them all out."

Since that was perfectly within her capabilities, Brenna still didn't see what was so funny, but she let it go. The shadows had lifted from Carson's eyes. However briefly such a thing might last, she wouldn't question it.

Suddenly conscious of biting her lip so hard it throbbed, she tilted her chin up and pretended intense fascination with the sun visor.

"Do you think that bar serves food?"

He glanced at his watch, a black-banded Timex. "Are you hungry already? We just ate breakfast."

She nodded. With the urge to change came fierce hunger, a strong need for red meat to sustain the body. Glad he hadn't noticed her inner struggle, she settled back in her seat.

Then Carson cast her the sort of sideways look males of all species can give, and she knew she hadn't entirely fooled him. He knew something was up. He just didn't know what it was.

"I'm starving." As if on cue, her stomach rumbled.

"It's a biker bar," he said. "A lot like the one upstate, where you found me. Greasy hamburgers are probably the best they have."

"A greasy hamburger sounds wonderful." She

meant every word. Her mouth watered thinking about it.

"And about the bar being safe, if any Hades' Claws are hanging out there, I doubt they'll expect us to walk right in among them. They're used to terrifying their prey. So going in there will probably be a lot safer than if we sat on the bench in front of our motel."

Unnerved by his use of the word *prey,* she nodded.

A few minutes later he made a right turn into an unmarked lot. "Here we are."

Barely four miles from the gated compound, towering pine trees surrounded the uneven parking lot. A faded, hand-painted sign hung on the weathered-gray building, proclaiming they'd arrived at a bar called— appropriately enough—Dante's.

If she were simply driving by, she wouldn't even take a second look, so unassuming was the structure. Most notable about the place was the way the winter sun reflected off row upon row of gleaming chrome handlebars and exhaust pipes. Only two cars and a pickup shared the parking lot with the sea of motorcycles.

"There must be fifty." Brenna couldn't take them all in. "When you said biker bar, you weren't kidding."

Flashing her another quick smile, he parked as far from the rows of bikes as the lot would allow.

"In case we have to make a quick getaway." This time his brittle smile took on a sharp edge.

Stepping from the Tahoe, Brenna inhaled deeply, searching for the scent of trouble. This time the chilly afternoon air carried only a vague promise of snow, nothing more. Cocking her head, she listened, but heard only the faint sound of music and raucous voices from inside the bar. Maybe Carson was right. Maybe Hades' Claws wouldn't bother them here, so close to their den. She bared her teeth. The violence of the urge to change had her spoiling for a fight.

"Are you okay?" Carson's deep voice broke into her thoughts. He'd been watching her. Again. Had she been too careless, revealed too much of her true nature? Chastising herself under her breath, she gave a curt nod. When he opened the heavy wooden door, she squared her shoulders and swept past him into the dim, smoky interior.

Wincing at the acrid odor of cigarette smoke, she glanced around. The rolling swagger with which she walked had taken weeks to perfect.

At her entrance, several men looked up with interest. Two of them immediately headed her way, their eyes gleaming. Neither noticed the other, so she braced herself for the inevitable clash when they both reached her at the same time.

Immediately Carson slung his arm across her shoulders and pulled her close. The possessive message was plain. *Back off.*

Both men stopped, sized Carson up and turned back to their companions.

Brenna turned to glare at Carson. "What the—"

"Shh." His breath warmly tickled her ear, sending a shiver down her spine. "I want them to know you're with me."

"I won't learn as much," she growled back. Still, she forced a smile. Odd how his touch seemed to be able to take her mind off the need to change. Usually nothing and no one could do that. The urge would lessen only once she'd given in.

"Hey, you look like you want to fight me. Relax," he said, keeping her close.

As if. Across the crowded room, she spied two empty chairs and a rickety round table. "There's a place."

"Great," he said. "We'll order a drink."

"I want something to eat," she reminded him. He left his arm around her as they slowly crossed the room. She found it much more difficult to do her stroll this way and, after two steps, gave it up. As they wound their way through the crowd, though some continued to watch them, most people paid them no mind.

Checking for danger, she continued to breathe deeply. Mingled with the yeasty scent of beer and ever-present cigarette smoke, the air smelled of male sweat. A quick glance around told her she was one of maybe five women to fifty or more men.

"Such odds," she murmured. "Ten men to every woman."

He leaned his head close, still carrying on the charade, she supposed. "Some women would like it." He licked her ear.

Damn the man. Even here, he could still make her knees go weak.

"Stop," she hissed. "Let go."

They'd reached their table and finally Carson released her. With a sigh, she dropped gratefully onto the hard wooden seat.

A waiter, his gray braid longer than Brenna's, leaned close. On his forearm he had a shotgun tattoo, and his hand bore the insignia of a large, hairy spider. This time her shudder was from distaste. She despised spiders.

"What d'ya want?"

"I'll have a hamburger." Steeling herself, she let her gaze wander over him, as though she found him attractive. He lifted an arm, and she discovered he'd neglected to put on deodorant that morning.

"And water," she added, unable to keep from wrinkling her nose at the odor.

"Budweiser." Beside her, Carson smelled it, too. She could tell from his choked tone.

The waiter managed to leer at Brenna and smile at the same time. "Gotcha. Be right back." He lurched off toward the bartender.

"Why'd you check him out?" Carson asked gruffly. "If you say he's your type, I'm outta here."

Was he making another joke? "Are you all right?"

He frowned. "Why?"

With a shrug, she lightly touched his hand. "Nothing. You seem different, that's all."

His frown deepened, making her sorry she'd mentioned his mood. Now he would probably revert to the surly, bitter Carson she knew.

"Thank you," he finally said, looking off into the roomful of people.

"For what?"

He leaned back, crossing one booted foot over his leg. She was struck by how well he fit in here, despite his lack of tattoos or earrings.

"For reminding me who I am. And who you are."

His words stung. "You're welcome," she retorted.

He continued to ignore her. She watched as he scanned the crowd.

Some demon drove her. "So…you forgot who I am?"

At first she didn't think he would answer. He didn't

turn his head, even when the waiter reappeared with his beer and her water. The few cubes of ice were already melting in the large plastic glass. Once the waiter had threaded his way to the next table, Carson took a long, deep drink of his beer. When he met her gaze, she saw that the self-reproach was back in his.

"I never forget," he said. "Anything."

His words sounded like a threat.

A moment later the waiter brought her hamburger. The tantalizing scent of meat drove all other thoughts from her mind. Seconds after he'd deposited the full plate in front of her, she grabbed the burger and began to devour it. Though she preferred meat slightly rare, and this had been cooked until it was nearly rubbery, she ate half in three bites, washing it down with gulps of lukewarm water.

Well on her way to finishing, she became conscious of Carson—and several other men—watching her eat. She ignored their avid interest—and Carson's speculative stare. She didn't much care if human women ate as quickly. The protein filling her blood with a rush of power felt good. The energy coursing through her—red meat, without the hunt—empowered her with optimism.

The hamburger went too quickly, so she started on the fries. Carson had barely finished half his beer by the time she'd cleaned her entire plate.

A reluctant smile pulled at one corner of his mouth. "Hungry?"

"I was." Smiling back, she licked her lips. His gaze, following her tongue, intrigued her. With fresh energy flowing through her veins, she felt the sensual connection between them much more strongly, supplanting even the ever-present urge to change.

His pupils darkened, and she knew he felt it, too. He leaned forward. She scooted her chair closer.

"Brenna—"

Behind them, glass shattered. She jumped. The entire room erupted. Men scrambled to their feet, a few heading for the door, more heading for the knot of bodies in the back corner of the room.

"Fight!" someone shouted.

Pushing back his chair so hard it clattered to the floor, Carson stood, blocking her view.

"Don't move," he ordered. "Things could get dangerous. I'll be right back." Pushing through the crush of bodies, he disappeared into the crowd.

For the space of two seconds she sat, staring after him. Shouts—egging the two combatants on—and the splintering sound of a chair breaking. Danger brought exhilaration, mingled with the trailing remnants of lust, all fueled by the fresh vigor in her blood.

No way she could simply sit and wait while everyone else got in on the action. She jumped to her feet, getting ready to duck and dodge in Carson's general direction, and found her way blocked by a tall, male form.

"'Scuse me." She attempted to skirt around him without making eye contact.

"Brenna," a deep and achingly familiar voice said, "what the hell are you doing?"

She froze. Looked up. And met brown eyes so much like her own. "Alex?"

Chapter 10

"Alex." Her heart thumped so hard she feared it might burst from her chest. "I can't... I've been—"

"Shh." He enfolded her in a tight hug. "You always worried too much."

Normally those were fightin' words. And he knew it.

She held on to his forearms with a death grip. "Where have you been? What have you done? You disappeared. You scared the hell out of me, you know. You'd better start talking."

A crash—the back corner again. Two more men ran to join the fray. Alex glanced back. Then, apparently satisfied that they weren't being observed, he shook his head in warning at Brenna. He wore his blond hair long, the cut shaggy. The shadow of a beard darkened his chin and cheeks. He looked like Brad Pitt gone bad.

"I don't have much time. Shh," he said, when she opened her mouth to speak. Tension radiated off him.

"I just need to know—"

"Questions can wait." He grimaced, his expression dark. "It's bad here right now. Deadly. I want you safe. Gone. Go home."

"But—"

"No." His eyes blazed. "Leave, Brenna. Now."

"Well, well, well." From behind them, a bitter voice. Carson. "I thought you might show."

Releasing Brenna, Alex turned to face the other man. Brenna noted Carson's set jaw, clamped mouth and intent gaze. Her brother's expressionless face she could not read.

Her insides clenched. Though it seemed as if she'd been waiting for this moment forever, the roiling emotions inside her made her feel ill.

Carson. Alex. She looked from her beloved brother to the man she'd come to care for.

"Not here," Alex said, his harsh words a clipped order. "Not in front of my sister."

Carson laughed. His hand hovered near his shoulder holster. Near his gun.

Both men glared at each other.

"You're coming with me," Carson growled. "I'm placing you under arrest."

"Don't pull your gun in here."

"If I have to—"

"No." Expression unchanged, Alex glanced once more around the crowded room. "I'm not going anywhere. Not yet. Not today. Friday we'll talk. I want you to get out of here. Take Brenna home."

"Brenna!" Carson exploded. "This isn't about your sister, damn you. This is about my wife, my little girl. I've been looking for you for eighteen months. I saw you there—the day Julie and Becky died. I saw you, Alex, you...my partner. You killed them, and then you tossed the gun away. Right after you shot me in the back.''

Chest tight, holding her breath, Brenna prayed for her brother to deny Carson's horrible accusations.

Instead, he shook his head, his narrow-eyed gaze revealing nothing.

''This is not the time to talk about what you think happened that day. Take Brenna home, Carson,'' Alex said. ''They meant to kill you then. They failed. You might not be so lucky this time. They want you dead. And they'll take my sister with you.''

''Lucky?'' The single word shook with rage. ''I want answers.'' Carson stood his ground, one hand now resting on the handle of his gun.

After glancing around once more to make sure the rest of the room remained occupied by the fight, Alex shook his head. His next words came in staccato bursts. ''Not now. It's big...huge. I'm on it, man. The killer— I'm gonna bring him down. Don't mess it up. And don't involve my sister.'' He took a step closer. ''Get her out of here before she gets hurt.''

''You're serious?'' Carson's lips twisted in an imitation of a smile. ''You expect me to believe you're worried about your sister when you can't even tell the truth about what happened?'' He looked at Brenna. ''How does it feel, knowing your brother is a cold-hearted murderer?''

She recoiled, still reeling from her brother's lack of defense. Carson's words stung.

''I'd like to beat some sense into both of you,'' she muttered. They both looked at her, Carson still expressionless, Alex registering a brief moment of surprise.

"Brenna—" Warning sounded clear in Alex's sharp tone. "You have no place in this."

"But I do." She touched her brother's shoulder lightly. "I'd like to see this settled. Let's go somewhere else and talk, someplace private."

"No time." He looked once more at the crowd still gathered in the back corner.

"You're coming with me." Carson's hand still rested on the pistol. "Under arrest. For murder."

A shout came from the back of the room. One of the combatants lifted a chair and bashed another on the head. The man crumpled to the ground. Shouting, several others moved in to restrain the first man. The fight was winding down.

Alex looked around them yet again, his actions furtive and earnest at the same time. He stared at Carson with such deadly intent that Brenna's entire body stilled.

"Shoot me, then," he growled, baring his teeth. "Shoot me and be done with it. But, buddy, if you do, you won't ever know the truth, will you?"

Carson drew his gun.

With a savage snarl, Alex stood his ground. "I didn't kill Julie and Becky. It wasn't me, damn you. But go ahead, shoot me now. Get it over with. Do you want the blood of the wrong man on your hands? Do you?" He poked Carson in the chest, hard.

His free hand clenched into a white-knuckled fist, Carson stood frozen, his expression shattered, and let him. Slowly, without taking his gaze from the other man's face, he holstered his pistol.

"I sure as hell don't," Alex said. His hard voice

cracked, and Brenna knew that no matter what had really happened that awful day, Alex blamed himself for Carson's loss.

As the fight broke up, the first wave of men scattered, returning to their seats or making for the exit. A man moved in front of Brenna, and for a moment she couldn't see Alex or Carson. Two or three more burly bikers shoved each other—and her. She pushed back, ignoring a challenging glare from one man, squeezing around another. When she could see Carson again, he stood alone. Alex had gone.

"Damn." Pushing a man out of his way, Carson turned and began elbowing his way to the door. Grabbing hold of his shirt, she followed in his wake, continually scanning the crowd in vain for a glimpse of her golden-haired brother.

Along with twenty or thirty others, they spilled out the door, trapped in the stream of exiting bikers.

Outside, dusk had fallen. Men congregated in the parking lot, laughing about the fight, standing around their gleaming motorcycles. There were bikers of every size, portly men in leather and short men in jeans. Long-haired and short, tall or thin, the crowd looked menacing. Brenna saw no sign of Alex.

"He's gone." Carson swore. "With this many people, we won't even find footprints in the snow."

"Look!" someone yelled, pointing toward the field across the road. At the edge of the snow-covered grass, where the tangle of forest began again, a large, silver wolf watched them, silhouetted in the approaching darkness.

"That's one big dog," another man commented. Someone whistled, and the animal lifted his massive head.

But Brenna knew the shadowy figure was not a dog. The wolf was her brother. Alex had changed. As they all watched, he turned and slipped into the underbrush.

Ignoring the latest commotion, Carson still scanned the crowd. Two men sidled up behind him. Distinctive snake tattoos decorated their forearms. Hades' Claws. She saw the glint of metal. One of them held a weapon in his hand.

Correctly recognizing the threat, Carson spun. Too slow. The metal edge of a knife glittered and slashed. He grunted in pain.

Brenna lunged forward. Arms came around from behind her, pinning her in place. Pretending to struggle, she twisted instead and dropped her shoulder, freeing herself. Out of his grip, she spun and aimed a hard kick at his shin. Violence—the scent of blood… Change. She felt an inner shifting. So it always began.

No. Not here. Not now.

Carson.

Another man blocked her. One swift chop and he went down. She pushed past him. Outnumbered, Carson tried to draw his gun. Another cut—like slow motion—knife raised, Carson's arm, wrist, a slash of crimson. Blood. The urge to change roared inside her. She froze, occupied momentarily by her own savage inner battle.

Carson grimaced, held on to the gun a moment longer, but the second man knocked it from him. It fell, clattering to the ground. The first attacker reached, and Carson kicked it away.

Blood. Carson's blood. She could smell the coppery scent of it. She took a step forward.

Change.

Again she fought the compulsion. The laws of the Pack were strict. She could not change now. Not here. There were far too many witnesses.

Still fighting, Carson swung. Missed. Grunted. An awful look on his face, he staggered. Straightened.

Internal battle won, she used her martial arts training. A twist, an elbow. She sprang forward. Picking himself up off the ground, one attacker took off, running. The other man followed suit.

No. She couldn't let them get away.

Change. The urge slammed into her.

She felt the change begin in her. With a snarl, she shook it off. With the energy rush giving her strength, she began to run. Half wild animal, with each pounding step she regained control of herself.

Someone shouted. Others came toward them. The two attackers rounded the corner of the building. The crowd surrounded Carson, blocking him from her view. Brenna stopped, breathing hard. Carson. She had to make sure he was okay. No one else must be allowed to hurt him.

Abandoning the chase, she went back, thrusting herself between him and the others.

"Give him room," she ordered. "Back off. Let him have space."

Carson still stood, his eyes bleary and hot and furious. The only signs of his pain were the deep furrows at the edge of his mouth. That, and the blood from the slash on his wrist.

She pushed back his jacket. The side of his shirt was sticky and crimson. Glaring at her, he held his hand pressed to his side.

"Someone call an ambulance," Brenna ordered.

When no one moved, she raised her voice. "An ambulance. Now."

"No hospital." Carson's jaw worked. He touched her arm. "It's not as bad as it looks."

She flashed him a look of disbelief. "You must be delirious."

"No." He shook his head. "It's not serious. A surface wound. Just get me out of here." He grimaced. "Please."

That simple word, more than anything else, made up her mind. He must be badly hurt. For now, she did as he asked, leading him across the parking lot, waving off the curiosity seekers who came to try and help or simply gawk.

A few scarlet drops had fallen on his boots, staining the leather. She wondered if he noticed. A quick glance at his set profile told her Carson was hurting far worse than he'd admitted.

"I'll drive." She struggled to get the rear passenger door open, succeeded, then helped him climb up. Leaning heavily on her shoulder, he breathed hard. She closed the door, went around to the driver's side, and once behind the wheel, held out her hand for the keys.

"Don't..." He swallowed and grimaced. "Don't go back to the motel. Not yet. I'm too vulnerable." He drew the key chain from his pocket and clumsily tossed it to her.

She caught it easily. "The motel? Are you crazy? We're going to the hospital."

After turning the key in the ignition, she backed out of the lot, zigzagging past the clustered knots of bikers. No one tried to stop her as she peeled out onto the road.

"No." He sat up. Winced. Lowered his voice. "No hospital."

Men. Pack or human, they were all the same. "Cut the macho crap. You're hurt."

"Not really." He lifted his hand, showing fingers covered with blood. Reaching into the glove box, he grabbed a few paper napkins, pressing them against his ruined T-shirt.

"I've had it. Really had it. Don't lie to me." Resisting the urge to bare her teeth, she allowed herself a furious growl.

"Don't worry about me. It's not your problem."

She glared at him. "I can't stand stupidity. This *is* my problem. *You* are my problem. You need medical help."

All at once the anger left him. The merciless planes of his face smoothed out. His mouth twisted in what Brenna guessed he must think looked like a smile. It resembled a smile as much as her low growl resembled a human sound. Not at all.

"No hospital," he said again. "I'm okay."

"Carson…" she warned.

"I'm not lying. It hurts like hell, but it's just a cut. Not much more than a scratch. I think it's almost stopped bleeding. No hospital. I don't trust anyone here."

"Fine." She sighed. "No hospital."

"Thank you.

"They stabbed you." Dividing her attention between the road and Carson, Brenna shuddered. The aftershocks of denying the need to change would last awhile. "Alex was right. They mean to kill you."

"Yeah. Probably on his orders."

"Get real. He warned us. He doesn't want you to get killed."

"Right," he drawled. "Let's see. I've been hunting the man for eighteen months, and he slips right by me. Then, while I'm preoccupied looking for him—bam. Knife to the ribs. Out of nowhere. I sure as hell didn't expect that. Carelessness nearly cost me my life." He sounded so disgusted that she nearly smiled. Nearly. But she was too wound up to smile much about anything.

"Alex is—"

"One of the bad guys," he interjected. "That's obvious."

"Obvious?" She clenched the wheel to keep from snarling. "It doesn't seem obvious to me. If he's one of them, then why would he risk himself to warn us?"

"You."

She looked sideways at him. "What?"

"He showed himself because of you. He's worried about you, about you being in danger. He didn't warn *us,* he warned *you.* Alex doesn't give a rat's ass about me."

"You're wrong. Did you see his face when he mentioned your family? Did you?" This time she did bare her teeth, just a little. "He's hurting, too, Carson. Having witnessed that, can you honestly say he doesn't care?"

His face contorted. "Stop the car."

"Like hell I will," she snarled back, matching his tone exactly. "Not until I think it's safe."

He leaned forward, maybe meaning to reach over the seat and grab for the wheel. But his sudden movement made him grimace. He gave a strangled cry, jerking up short.

"That was stupid, dammit. I ripped my side wide open." He fell back in the seat. "Now it's bleeding again."

Brenna's stomach clenched. She wanted to pull the Tahoe over right then, so she could assess the extent of his injury. Instead, she lifted her chin and forced herself to drive on, staring straight ahead at the road, trying to calm the churning inside her.

"He killed my family." Carson's voice was thick.

The pain she heard in his tone made her wince. Still, she had to defend her brother. "You don't know what happened. You didn't see. How do you know who shot them?"

"Maybe I don't, but he let them die." His expression was bleak. "I don't remember much of what happened that night, especially after I was shot. My cover had been blown and I didn't even know it. But Alex stayed with the gang, still undercover. How was my cover blown when his wasn't?"

She didn't answer.

"He had to know what they meant to do."

"I'm sure he didn't or he would have stopped it." She eyed Carson, letting conviction round out her voice. "I know Alex. He would never have done such a thing or allowed it to happen if he knew. I'm surprised you can think so, if you were as close as you say."

"I told you. I saw him holding the gun. The pistol that killed my wife and little girl. He was there. He shot them. It was a test, a test for him to prove his loyalty. If he failed, they wouldn't have let him stay in the Claws."

She shook her head. "I don't believe it."

"Believe this—he disappeared." Self-recrimination

showed in the deep lines on the sides of his mouth. "I was in the hospital a long time. Nearly died. When I found out Julie and Becky were gone, I went a little crazy. By the time I—" He shook his head, raw emotion glittering in his dark eyes.

Chest tight, Brenna looked away. "I'm so sorry," she murmured. "I can't imagine—"

"My wife never knew," he said softly. "She didn't suffer. At least, that's what they told me. They shot her from behind, one shot, straight through the back into her heart. She died instantly. Didn't even have time to scream."

Brenna's throat ached. "Your daughter?" She heard herself whisper.

"I can't talk about my daughter." His voice cracked. "She was only five."

He took several deep breaths. When he spoke again, his tone was flat and unemotional.

"Alex made no effort to contact me. Today was the first time I've seen him in a year and a half."

There were no words she could speak to ease his pain. Blinking back the tears that stung her eyes, tears he would hate, she simply gripped the steering wheel and drove.

"There." He pointed to an unmarked road that led directly west, into the setting sun.

She slowed the Tahoe and turned. After a few hundred feet, the pavement became dirt. They plowed on ahead. The road was full of potholes and ruts. They bounced, and more than once bottomed out. Carson groaned, and Brenna saw he'd gone white.

On one side of the road, a grassy shoulder led to an old, untended cemetery. Coasting to a stop in front of the haphazard stone fence, she shifted into Park and killed the engine. With a sigh, she opened the driver's door and went around to the back. Leaning in toward him, she nearly laughed out loud at the puzzled look he gave her.

"Let me see it." She pointed toward his side.

His expression shuttered, he slowly shook his head. "I'm fine."

Carefully keeping her face impassive, she gave him the sort of look mothers all over the world could relate to. "Let me see the damn wound."

His slight recoil made her want to smile. She didn't.

"I'm fine," he repeated.

Ignoring him, she slowly pried away the hand he kept pressed against the bunched-up and bloody shirt.

"It's a clean slice." Only by pretending he was like the injured animals she'd treated in the past could she objectively examine the cut. Carson had told the truth. It was a narrow slice, not deep enough to have caused serious damage.

"Yeah." His voice sounded distant. "Hurts like hell."

"We need to get some disinfectant." Matter-of-factly she ripped away a clean part of his T-shirt, then folded and pressed it into his gash. "No telling where that knife had been."

This elicited a grim smile. "I don't see a drugstore anywhere around here. So unless you happen to carry around a bottle of hydrogen peroxide in your purse, I'd say we're out of luck."

"No first-aid kit?"

He shook his head. "Didn't care."

Brenna thought of the Pack and the way wolves licked their injuries to clean them. She sighed, envisioning Carson's horrified reaction were she to suggest such a thing.

"I'll be fine," he told her, again giving her the eerie feeling he had read her mind. "It's just about stopped bleeding again."

She glanced around to get her bearings. The spot she had chosen was not only isolated but deserted. Not even a single house could be seen through the thick tangle of leafless tree limbs.

A perfect place for a wolf to run. She pushed the thought away.

"Did you pick this place for a reason?" He indicated the tumbled gravestones, some of which were so ancient the engraving had been wiped clean by time. "Is this a hint?"

This time, she let herself smile. "No hint. If I'd wanted you dead, I would have killed you a long time ago."

He whistled, giving her a long, slow perusal. "You sound like you mean it."

"I do," she said. "What now? You said no hospital, and you don't want to go back to the motel." The deepening purple of the sky told her night would soon be upon them. Without a single streetlight, their parking spot by the cemetery would be dark indeed. She looked again at the jumble of tombstones, unease prickling under her skin.

"Maybe this isn't a good place to stop," she said.

"We'll sleep in the Tahoe."

The back of her neck tingled. Not a good sign. No telling what other sorts of beings might roam such a deserted cemetery in the deep part of night. Though she had never met a vampire, she knew they were out there. She had no desire to meet one now, with Carson fairly reeking of blood.

And, more important for her, being this close to nature would intensify the desire to change. She was struggling enough with that as it was.

Of course, she could tell him none of those reasons.

"You know," she said, keeping her voice casual, "I really think we should go back to the motel. We've already made it plain we're not leaving."

Immediately he shook his head. "Too easy. Let them think I'm scared. Or seriously hurt. Whatever. We need to throw them off a little. That'll buy me time to come up with a plan."

"I thought you had a plan."

"Things have changed. I need a better one."

Because he'd seen Alex. Clearly that hadn't gone the way he'd expected.

"I think you need stitches."

He lifted his hand from his side. "I'm fine."

She gave up. She supposed another scar on his body wouldn't matter. Why should it, when he already had so many scars on the inside?

"Your call," she said.

"My call? Fine. We sleep here."

She studied him. The stark beauty of his profile, silhouetted in the waning sun of winter, made her ache. Even now, seated so close to her, he had an air of isolation that seemed almost physical.

She couldn't stand it. Wolves ran in packs. A solitary animal was unheard of. How could she make Carson understand he was no longer alone? She was with him now. Suddenly, fiercely, she wanted to break through his barrier and touch him, really *touch* him. More deeply than merely her fingers on his skin.

Glancing at him, she saw he was watching her.

"Brenna..." The warning in the way he spoke her name told her he somehow knew. No longer caring, she climbed in and scooted close, heart thudding in her chest, never taking her gaze from his face.

With a sound—a cry of resistance?—he reached out and met her halfway. Though no doubt meant to stop her, his touch felt oddly gentle. His hands tight on her shoulders, he held her off, but for only an instant; then he slowly slid his hands down her arms to bring her closer.

"Brenna," he said again, breathing hard. At first she thought the movement had caused him pain. Then a quick glance at his fully aroused body assured her that what he felt was an entirely different type of pain.

He spoke her name again, and she understood this was his way of giving her a second chance. She could pull away now if she wanted. Pull away? She would sooner die. Instead, she leaned into him and moved her lips over his, openmouthed, an invitation.

With a groan he captured her mouth with his, hard, demanding and...searching? Yearning. Or was that only in her head, a projection of her own emotions onto him? She didn't care.

Both trembling, they kissed, tongues intertwined, bodies straining. Passion arced between them, as strong and as violent as the winter lightning that sometimes rent the sky. She let her bewilderment, anger, confusion fuse into this one point of contact, mouth to mouth, Carson to Brenna, mate to mate.

Mate to mate? No! This was nothing so serious, no bonding, no binding, not mating at all.

Fighting panic, she raised her head. He grabbed her hair and pulled her back, claiming her with a deep, searing kiss. He drank of her, taking her essence into him and exchanging his own. Such a thing, new and fascinating, thrilled her, making her already-overloaded senses reel.

Mate? No, this couldn't be what it felt like, couldn't be what it seemed. Animal instinct, nothing more.

To her mingled relief and disappointment, Carson finally lifted his mouth from hers. The cadence of his harsh breathing matched her own.

"We'd better stop." He ground out the words, his eyes smoky with a heat equal to hers.

She didn't answer, not so readily capable of speech as he, afraid that if she opened her mouth she would end up begging him to make love to her. Instead she jerked her head in a tiny nod, wondering why she felt such an aching sense of loss.

Chapter 11

Carson decided that he needed to get Brenna to go. Anything to keep his already overheated body from reacting to her incredible sensual lure.

Damn. Now was one hell of a time for his libido to go into overdrive.

Closer to finding his family's killer than he'd ever been, so near to the end he could taste the sharp, metallic tang of victory, Brenna was a distraction he could ill afford. If he were a different man or a less cynical one, he would have laughed out loud at the bitter irony.

Instead he found himself wanting to weep.

Damaged in so many more ways than the small stab wound in his side, he had no right to take what Brenna so passionately offered. Not now, not ever. Used up, hollow, he had nothing to give in exchange. The quick fix of a one-night stand would create more problems than it would solve. Despite her self-sufficient attitude and attempts to appear tough, Brenna was a forever kind of girl. An emotionless, no-strings-attached, sexual encounter would hurt her. His wife had been the same way.

Brenna shifted, running her hand through her long, dark hair. Watching, he realized he knew the exact texture of each smooth strand. He thought how erotic a silken curtain her hair would make, cascading over them when they made love.

When? How about *if* they made love?

No. They would not make love. Ever. He shook his head, tearing his gaze away from her. Damn! He still wanted her. Badly. He groaned out loud.

"Are you all right?" Her concerned expression told him she'd mistaken his frustration for a sound of pain.

"Yeah, I'm fine." Steeling himself, he gave a pointed glance at the front seat. "If we're going to sleep tonight, one of us needs to move up front. It's crowded back here."

"Crowded?" Her cool tone matched his. She studied his face, probably trying to figure out what made him tick. He couldn't blame her. One minute he was all over her, the next he couldn't get far enough away.

Tough. Squaring his shoulders, he looked at the growing darkness outside the window. He couldn't afford to get distracted—not by her, not by anything. He knew what mattered. Finding the killer, whether Alex or some other man. Finding him and bringing him to justice. Nothing else.

His priorities firmly back in place, Carson refused to watch as she started to scramble forward between the two front seats. He was admiring her perfect rear end—in the abstract, of course—when she appeared to have second thoughts.

After a pause, she moved into the driver's seat, fastened her seat belt with a click, then started the engine and pulled onto the road, tires spinning, all without even once looking at him.

"What the—"

"We're going back to the motel." Her no-nonsense tone told him she meant it. "Phelan will need to go out, and he'll need to be fed."

He'd forgotten about the puppy. "We'll get him and take him with us."

This time she did look at him, a quick, hard stare that told him not to give her any flak. "We're staying there. I don't like this graveyard."

Suddenly tired, he didn't feel like arguing. He had to try, anyway. "I told you, the motel isn't safe."

"Is anywhere? I mean, come on. This gang seems to know where we're gonna be before we do."

He sat bolt upright, causing another painful pull to his side. "I can't believe I didn't think of that."

"Of what?" Her exasperated tone told him that she still wasn't buying whatever he had to say.

"A tracking device." He didn't bother searching the inside of the Tahoe. It had to be in a wheel well or underneath. When they stopped again, he would find the damn thing and yank it off. "They're tracking us."

"Sure they are." Now she sounded as though she thought he was delusional. "And maybe little green men are hiding under the seats."

Though he really shouldn't care what she thought, for some reason her snide comment rankled him.

"Even your brother said they weren't taking any

chances I'd get near them," he reminded her. "This way they can be sure."

Silence while she digested his words. Finally she gave a slow nod. "Alex is usually right," she said.

He hated that it took a mention of Alex to make her pay attention.

Back at the motel, they both emerged from the Tahoe in silence. His side aching like hell, ten times worse than he let on, Carson bent over to inspect the undercarriage of the vehicle.

"What does a tracking device look like?" she asked.

Straightening, he dragged his hand across his dry mouth. His rib cage was on fire. Perspiring heavily for no good reason, he straightened. The entire world swayed and tilted on its axis.

"It could look like anything." He heard himself speaking as if from a distance. "Most likely—"

He saw a burst of black; then the ground rushed up to meet him.

Change of scenery. Inside the motel room. Ugly green shag carpet. Unmade bed and lumpy pillow. How much time had passed? Confused, he tried to lift his head, and the room spun.

"I'll bet that hurt." Brenna's voice, soothing and low, sounded close to his ear.

Swallowing, he opened his eyes and found her. "What happened?"

Her expression seemed grim. "You passed out. I had to drag you inside."

She was lying. Had to be. No way could she, all of five feet tall and a hundred pounds soaking wet, manage to move his bulk.

"Who helped you?"

Ignoring the pain in his side, he watched the emotions flit across her face. Worry, confusion, frustration, then, finally, comprehension.

"You don't think I could have moved you by myself." Not a question. She wasn't stupid. She knew it would be a Herculean task, even for a much larger female. He said nothing, waiting.

"I'm very strong." Color stained her cheeks. He wondered why she would lie to him, especially after what had just happened. Then a thought hit him, a possibility so infuriating that he pushed himself up on his elbows to glare at her.

"Alex?"

Instantly her entire posture changed to one of watchful alertness. "What about Alex?"

"No." He had to grind his teeth to keep from shouting. "Did your brother help you get me inside?"

"Of course not." She waved his suggestion away, shaking her head and sending her dark hair flying. "No one helped me."

Another thought, equally plausible, equally bad. "The guys in the room next door? The federal agents? Damn." Surprised he wasn't in handcuffs, he let himself fall back onto the pillow, rubbing his eyes to clear the cobwebs. The blackness receded, then surged again, causing him to keep himself immobile, fighting to keep from drifting in and out of consciousness.

When he opened his eyes, Brenna had moved away. He could hear her rustling through a plastic bag on the other side of the room. With an effort he managed to lift his head and next, his aching shoulders. With his elbows for support, he struggled to sit up again.

"Here." She propped two pillows behind his back. "Maybe this will help."

He didn't thank her. Since even his own traitorous body wanted to betray him, he fought the grayness and concentrated on the fiery ache in his side.

"Aspirin?" He croaked the word with a grimace. He still meant to find out how she had gotten him inside, though right now all his efforts were focused on not passing out.

"Here." She brought him three pills and dropped them into his palm, then handed him a can of diet cola. "I still think we need to go to the hospital."

"Where's your dog?" Deliberately changing the subject, Carson choked down the aspirin, washing them down his dry throat with the lukewarm cola.

Recognizing the word *dog,* the small animal placed his front paws on the side of the bed, cocking his head in enquiry.

"Have you fed him?" Carson let the puppy sniff his hand, then lick. "Has he been out?"

She flashed a smile. "Yes, he's eaten. How's your side?"

"Better. What about the dog?"

"He needs to go outside. I'll take care of him in a moment. Carson, we ought to have a doctor look at you."

"No." Squinting, he tried for a hard stare. "Pack up your stuff. We're leaving."

"You're delusional." She expelled her breath with a noisy puff. "If we're going anywhere, we're going to the hospital."

"I'll take the dog out."

"You can barely stand."

"I'm fine." He swung his legs over the side of the

bed, ignoring the crazy tilt the room took at the movement. "And we're not going to a hospital. Since you don't want to sleep in the Tahoe, we're changing motels. This one's not safe."

She stared at him, her expression unreadable. "Give me a realistic rationale, and I might agree. Otherwise, no."

"I've given you plenty of reasons."

"I don't think there's another motel in this town."

"We'll find one."

A reluctant smile tugged at her full lips. "Whatever you say. Did you find a tracking device?"

"No." He watched her closely. "Did you?"

"I didn't look." She gave a shrug, oddly graceful. "But I wouldn't know what to look for."

"Hmm. Tell me who helped you move me inside."

She froze. As he had intended, throwing the question at her from nowhere ambushed her. Maybe now he would get a straight answer.

"I need to know where I stand," he pushed. "If Alex is helping you, or if you've alerted the Feds that I'm here, I deserve to know."

"Alex didn't help me. And I didn't ask the men next door." Standing rigid, head held high, she met his gaze with a frank look of her own. "I'm telling you the truth. I dragged you in here by myself."

Next she would expect him to believe she could fly. Right.

"You heard my own agency warn me away from this investigation. They could be trying to stop us," he reminded her.

"I told you, I didn't even talk to those guys."

He tried another tack. "How long was I out?"

"Long enough," she said. "I didn't time you."

"Fine." He would accept that for now, since she gave him no other choice. "Get your stuff."

Pushing himself to his feet, he stood, swaying slightly. He gripped one side of the bed for support. Hoping she wouldn't notice, he squared his shoulders. "We'll take the dog out together."

"Phelan," she said, and shook her head. "He has a name. You might try using it."

Ignoring her, he opened the motel room and went outside. Brenna and her pet followed.

Though Brenna had been right about the lack of lodging, they'd finally found a small place on the other edge of town and gotten a room. After a quick meal of more greasy takeout, they'd showered—separately. Then, exhausted and hurting, he'd taken a couple more aspirin and dropped into a deep, dreamless sleep, for once not tossing and turning all night.

The deep sleep seemed to have helped. The next morning Carson woke feeling almost normal. The night before they'd picked up some bandages and antiseptic at a local pharmacy and doctored his side. Now the bleeding had stopped and the pain had subsided to a steady ache. He stretched, then grimaced at the sharp jab in his side. As long as he didn't make any sudden moves, he would be all right. He'd been lucky.

He'd also searched the Tahoe both inside and out, finding nothing. Maybe he'd been wrong about the tracking device; more likely he hadn't found it yet. Still, he was glad he'd insisted they change motels.

In the bed next to him, Brenna still slept. For a moment he studied the even motion of her chest, her glossy hair fanned out on the white pillow. Somehow, some way, she'd managed to get under his skin. Last night he'd dreamed of her. Startling thought, but he remembered the dream vividly. After all, he'd awoken from it hard and aching. Wanting her.

And, he realized as let himself drink in her sleeping form, he still ached with desire. He wanted to crawl under the sheets and roam his hands over her soft, pale skin, explore her slender shape. As he contemplated doing exactly that, guilt gnawed at him, reminding him once again how easily Brenna was able to distract him.

He shook his head, deliberately moving in a way that brought him fresh pain from his cut. Pain, in this case, might serve a good purpose, that of keeping him focused and on track.

She shifted, and the cadence of her breathing changed. Any moment she would open those big brown eyes and blink sleepily up at him, hair tousled.

At the thought, his body stirred again. Maybe a cold shower would be a good idea.

He sat up, once more welcoming the stab of pain, and slowly swung his legs over the side of the bed.

Phelan poked his head out from under Brenna's covers.

Tongue lolling out of his mouth, he appeared to be grinning. About to reach out and ruffle the dog's fur, Carson reconsidered. Such softness was more than he could stand right now. And touching the pup would bring his hand too close to the temptation of Brenna's body. So he stood, hating his unsteady wobble, and made his way into the bathroom for a much-needed cold shower.

The soft click of the bathroom door, followed by

the flush of the commode and the shower starting, brought Brenna fully awake.

Carson. She smiled, remembering the soul-searing intensity of the kiss they'd shared. Then frowned as she realized the direction her thoughts were taking.

With a heavy sigh she pushed back the blanket and discovered Phelan. Tugging at the sheet, the puppy wiggled mischievously. He wanted to play tug of war with the bedding.

Brenna laughed. Such wonderful innocence, so much like the young cublets in the Pack, made her long for her own childhood. Made her long to be—

A tremor shook her. Even being around the puppy increased the desire to change. The triggers were becoming more frequent, the need more consuming. She shook herself in frustration, gritting her teeth. This was the longest she'd remained totally human. Yet she had no choice. Somehow, until she'd settled things with her brother, she would have to suppress the urge. If she could.

The shower cut off, and a few minutes later Carson emerged. This time he wore only his jeans—not just a towel, hounds help her, as she didn't know how she would be able to keep from jumping his too-sexy-for-his-own-good bones then. Still, bare-chested, he looked good. Without looking at her, he crossed the room to his duffel bag. She couldn't keep from staring as he tugged his T-shirt over his head. Her mouth went dry even as she called herself names—dumb Brenna, really dumb. He used his fingers to comb out his still-damp hair.

Something about the quiet domesticity of the scene lifted her heart and brought an unfamiliar happiness.

He caught her watching and raised a brow. "What?"

"Nothing," she said, unable to keep from grinning. "I was just thinking something good is going to happen today."

He paused and studied her. "Any particular reason?" His casual tone told her the question was anything but.

"No." She gave a slow shake of her head. "But enough bad stuff has happened to us that I think the universe has got to cut us some slack."

"It doesn't work like that." One corner of his mouth twisted. Turning away, he grabbed the remote. Brenna indulged herself, admiring the view from the rear.

He clicked on the television. A diet cola commercial with a loud, inane jingle came on. Channel up. The local news anchor excitedly described a fire. Camera footage panned in on a roaring blaze. The building collapsed as they watched, despite the fire department's attempt to save it.

"That's the motel we were staying in until last night." Brenna stared, her heart beginning to pound. "I don't believe it."

Carson swore. "They torched it. They must have thought we were still there." He thumbed up the volume.

"At least two known dead," the news woman intoned. "Several more injured."

"Maybe I was wrong about the tracking device," Carson said slowly. "Obviously they didn't know we'd moved."

"The federal agents." Unable to peel her gaze

away from the television, Brenna's eyes ached. "Do you think they made it out?"

"If they didn't, Hades' Claws will have hell to pay. The Justice Department doesn't take kindly to the murder of their own."

Witnesses claimed they'd seen nothing. Heard nothing.

Most had been awakened by their smoke alarms going off.

"We need to put a stop to this." Brenna stood, tearing her gaze away from the screen to meet Carson's eyes.

"Oh, yeah?" He lifted a brow. "How do you propose to do that? Have you got a cadre of men with AK-47's that I don't know about?"

"No." Glancing back at the news, she bared her teeth, knowing Carson couldn't see. "But there has to be some way."

"When you think of one, let me know."

Another commercial came on. Carson stabbed the Off button. The sudden silence seemed poignant—and threatening.

Brenna exhaled. Inhaled. Repeated the process. She had to strive for calm, especially now. The momentary instant of violent rage that had bubbled up inside her had triggered her body to begin the onset of change. Each time, the craving intensified. Each time, subjugation proved more difficult.

Too bad. She had more important things to think about right now.

"So what's your plan?" she asked.

Carson took his time answering, rotating his neck while massaging the back of it. "I don't have one," he said. The stark words sounded bleak.

"It's got to get better," she repeated. "It certainly couldn't get any worse."

His grim expression told her that he thought it could. "Don't tempt fate."

As if on cue, Carson's cell phone rang. Keeping his back to her, he answered. The conversation was brief. She could only make out a few of his monosyllabic replies.

He snapped the phone closed. His sudden tension indicated the information he'd received hadn't been good. With a major effort of will, she waited.

"You were right about one thing." He flashed her a humorless smile. "Something good *is* going to happen today—for you. You're going home."

For one heart-stopping second she thought he meant something had happened to Alex. But no, his savage expression contained no satisfaction, just anger.

"Only if you go with me." She smiled, knowing he would do no such thing. "And since we've covered this before, I'm not going anywhere."

"You've got to leave," he said. "It's too dangerous for you. If you won't listen to me, listen to your brother. He warned you. He was right. Pack your stuff. I'll take you to catch a bus."

Her heart stuttered. "Was that Alex on the phone just now?"

"No." Jaw clenched, he bit out the single word. "That was Jack."

"Your informant?"

"Yeah." His hooded gaze was bleak. "Only, this time he said he had a message for me from the Claws."

"They know he talks to you?"

"Apparently so."

Moving forward, she touched his arm. "He's in trouble, then."

To her surprise, though he went very still, he didn't shake off her hand.

"More than trouble. This isn't like some TV show. He has something to tell me. He thinks they're on to him. I'm meeting him at the bus station in an hour. He's got to get out of town, too, or he's a dead man."

Chapter 12

Her hand on his arm felt like a brand. When she touched him, Carson froze. They had sixty minutes before they had to meet Jack. Suddenly, fiercely, he wanted to make love to her, take her swiftly, furiously, mindlessly.

Her small hand on his arm wasn't nearly enough. He could cover her hand with his, slide his palm up her arm to her shoulder, then cup her chin. One step would do it. One step, one move, and he could have her in his arms, where he could kiss her senseless. One touch, one kiss, would be enough to make both of them temporarily forget about this mess.

The light floral scent she wore made him think of Easter in the dead of winter. Renewal. The phone call, Jack's panicked voice, had brought everything into focus, made his emotions, desires and needs more intense. Enough was enough. He was tired of death. Once, just once, he longed to celebrate life.

The ache in his side felt inconsequential now. The cramped room, the trouble with Jack, all of it faded as he contemplated giving in to his newly awakened, raging libido and taking her, hard and fast and furious.

"What did Jack find out?" Brenna's worried voice broke through his thoughts.

Jack. He'd always tried to take care of him, slipping the kid a little extra so he could eat. How could he think of sex when Jack was in trouble? Furious at himself, he moved away. Though they had an hour, he needed to use the time to figure out a way to help Jack, to make sure he got out of town safely. Since Jack had been helping him, the younger man's trouble was now his responsibility, his fault.

"Hello, Carson?" Brenna repeated. "What about Jack's message?"

His priorities finally in order, he swallowed and hoped she wouldn't notice his raging arousal. He edged toward the bathroom.

"I think he's worried about you. He warned me to get you out of here. You're next, he said. His voice was shaking. First time I've ever heard him rattled."

"He's young." Her voice had gone soft, similar to the gentle way she spoke to Phelan. When she noticed Carson looking at her, she started toward him. Out of reflex, he stepped back, ignoring the pang he felt at hurting her. Then she lifted her chin, eyes flashing, and he told himself he'd only imagined it.

"We've known all along they're after me." He held up a hand to prevent her from moving. "And Jack, too, because of me. Now they want you, too. They'll kill you, do you understand? *That girl*, Jack specifically said."

"Why?" Her clipped tone showed anger, which surprised him. He would have expected fear. "Did they give a reason?"

She constantly surprised him. Most women would have reacted with fear. But then, nothing about Alex's sister was ordinary.

"It's like I've been telling you all along. You're with me. You might be my girlfriend, for all they know. You might know too much. Who knows how the hell they think? Most of them are borderline psychopaths."

"Psychopaths?" She sounded disbelieving.

"Yeah. Most killers are. So pack your stuff. I'll dress and then take you to the bus station. Jack thinks I should put you on the bus with him." He headed for the bathroom again.

"It could be a trap to distract you. They want you more than me."

He didn't turn around. "Could be. But that doesn't change anything. You're leaving."

She didn't reply. Maybe she finally understood. Hah—that would be a good one. He closed the bathroom door, sagging against it. Through Brenna hadn't seemed to notice, the front of his jeans still bulged conspicuously. Muttering to himself, he ran a hand through his longish hair.

"Ready?" he called, opening the door. "The bus station is downtown, near Main Street. If you need bus fare, I have it."

"Quit it." Crouched over, stroking Phelan, she didn't raise her head to look at him. He noticed she'd twisted her hair into a knot on the back of her head.

"I'm not going anywhere."

He should have known. "But—"

"Carson. I'm staying. Live with it."

Her casual choice of words cut deep. "I can't live with it, Brenna. There's no way I can live with another death on my hands."

She lifted her head and rose, graceful in tight jeans. Barefoot, she padded over to him. Before he understood what she meant to do, she wrapped her arms around him—careful of his side wound—and laid her head against his shoulder.

He tensed—couldn't help it—and tried to summon up the strength, the desire, to push her away. He couldn't find it. So he stood, frozen, knowing she could feel the proof of his desire for her. He waited for her to speak. When she didn't, merely held on, he breathed in her scent. Brenna. She'd somehow stormed her way inside his heart.

He should have felt angry. He should have felt miserable. Instead, he felt a dawning sense of wonder. She made him feel as though he had a future to anticipate, as if he still had hope. Such possibilities shouldn't exist—not in the gray aftermath of his bleak world. Since he knew them to be utterly, completely false, the very thought hurt a thousand times worse.

Still, he couldn't summon up the necessary will to make her release him. Maybe he'd become a masochist of sorts, for in the midst of such pain he found a bright blossom of pleasure.

Brenna.

How long they stood that way, he didn't know. Forever. Not long enough. Then, with a soft sigh, she finally released him. Silently moved away. Now, his weakness revealed, he couldn't bring himself to look at her, to meet her eyes. He'd stupidly made himself vulnerable, and there was no way he could deal with the pity he was sure to see. And pity she must feel. Compassion could be the only reason for her tenderness, though he'd certainly done nothing to deserve it.

Not quite steady, he tried to regain control of himself. The scent of flowers—roses? tulips?—lingered, out of place in the dingy hotel room. In the course of his job he'd stayed in a hundred similar places, each of them impersonal, a stopping place, a bed to sleep in. How he'd longed for home then, the brightness of his family's laughter and the comfort of knowing he was loved. He'd known how lucky he was each time he returned to the aroma of fresh-baked bread and his daughter's soft kisses, though he'd never truly appreciated the scope of his blessings. Not until they were savagely ripped from him.

Afterward, while he'd lain in his hospital bed willing himself to die, he'd had one question. The same question that surely plagued every other person who walked away from a fiery car crash, the lone survivor. Why? Why them and not him? Why had he lived while they died? Why?

Unable to find an answer, he'd finally gained some measure of understanding. He must have lost them because he'd never deserved them to begin with.

"Let's go save Jack," Brenna said, bright-voiced, as if nothing untoward had occurred.

He glanced at his watch. "We have forty-five minutes. I'll take the dog out before we go."

"Phelan." Her quiet tone rebuked him. "His name is Phelan."

"Fine. Whatever." He grabbed his jacket. In the small room, with her scent still fresh in his lungs, he felt uneasy. Maybe, if he went outside and breathed in deeply, the sharp air of the winter afternoon might clear his head.

If he let the scattered patches of unmelted snow dampen the bottom of his boots, he might be able to remember what was most important. Justice. Vengeance. Not gentle brown eyes and soft skin. Not a beguiling smile and come-hither body.

He spun, meaning to scoop up the puppy and go. But Phelan had heard Brenna say his name and was right there, under Carson's foot. He stumbled, the puppy yelped, and Brenna rushed over. They both bent at the same time to comfort the young dog, heads nearly colliding.

The front window shattered. Something hit the carpet, rolling into the bathroom. A second, a heartbeat. Carson recognized the oddly shaped gray cylinder— a pipe bomb.

"Down!" He jumped on Brenna, pushing her to the floor and covering her body and Phelan's with his own.

The world exploded.

After that, time existed only in flashes.

Searing heat. Fire. Move. He scooped up the shocked puppy, grabbed Brenna's arm. Smoke. Couldn't see. Burning.

Flames reached for them, attempting to lick at their jeans, hair, skin. Hurt.

Stop, drop and roll. No time. Need air.

More smoke. Heavy and blistering. More heat. Fire. Frantic, he sought a way out. An exit. There. An opening where the wall had been. Furious, hungry, the fire roared in front of them, behind them, surrounding them. Death.

Brenna clutched his hand. He caught a glimpse of her face. Her eyes were red and wide with terror.

"Jump," he shouted, throat raw. "Our only chance. Now!"

Together they leaped.

Then they were through. Free. Outside.

Run. He felt each footstep as they pounded the ground. Lungs burning, he sucked in air, cool and fresh. He rubbed his eyes. They were full of soot.

Brenna stayed with him. In the shimmering mirage caused by the heat, her movements seemed animal-like, powerful. Alien.

He didn't care. *Live,* he silently urged her, urged himself. *Live.* His heart pumped, pounded. Proof of life.

The sharp bite of icy air seared his lungs. Still running. Away from the motel. He'd parked the Tahoe around back, out of sight.

In the distance, sirens screamed.

Run.

At the edge of the trees, he collapsed. Brenna dropped to the wet ground beside him, coughing. Phelan whimpered, struggling to be free. Carson let him go, and the puppy staggered a few feet before dropping to the ground.

"Is he—"

Brenna crawled forward. She ran her hands over Phelan's immobile body. "He's all right, except his fur." Her voice sounded like sandpaper. She combed her fingers through the dog's short coat. "Singed."

"Check yourself," Carson ordered, discovering he, too, was unable to speak above a hoarse whisper. "For cuts. Burns."

He coughed, causing a sharp jab of pain in his side.

The knife wound. Minor. Ignoring it, he pushed himself to his knees and crawled over to Brenna, hacking and wheezing like an old man.

Damp and clammy, the ground was still snowy in spots, though mostly from old moldering leaves and mud. The numbing moisture felt good on the palms of his hands, dampening his jeans at the knees.

He couldn't seem to stop coughing.

"Are you okay?" She squinted at him.

When he could speak again he managed a nod. "Getting the smoke out of my lungs."

Though the night air felt crisp, he removed his jacket and spread it on the ground for her. "Here. Sit."

Once she was settled, he dropped down next to her. Phelan had staggered away, sniffing. He seemed intent on exploring the trees.

Brenna straightened and opened her mouth. Now she coughed, the spasms doubling her over. Feeling awkward, he reached out, patting her back. She jerked away, glaring at him, still hacking. Finally she wiped her mouth with the back of her hand.

"They found us," she said.

He nodded.

"Maybe we should go to the police."

"You know we can't."

"Phelan," she called. "Phelan."

The sirens grew louder. Across the field, a fire engine raced into the parking lot, lights flashing white and red.

His stomach clenched, remembering another time, another ambulance. That time help had come too late to save his family.

Brenna touched his arm, bringing him back to the present. "What do you want to do?"

"The Tahoe," he said. "It's all we have. We've got to get to it now."

She nodded and pushed herself to her feet, staggering slightly. Joints protesting, Carson did the same.

More sirens—police cars following the ambulance and fire truck. It wouldn't be long until the Feds from their last motel showed up, if they were still alive. If not, there would be others. Since a bomb had been used, ATF would be called in, as well. That meant DEA, FBI, ATF, as well as local and state police, would be swarming the place. Exactly what he—and, he would have thought, Hades' Claws—wanted to avoid.

A crowd began to gather in front of the burning motel. More cars raced up—most likely curious civilians—and pulled into the parking lot. Others stopped on the shoulder of the road, onlookers emerging to gawk at the inferno. Now, before the rest of the circus started, would be their only chance.

"Wait here," he said. She nodded, and he sprinted for the Tahoe. Gasping for air, he felt the beating his lungs had just taken. But he made it to the edge of the parking lot, slowing his pace, pretending to be another curiosity seeker watching the fire. Hoping the firefighters were too intent on the blaze to notice him, he unlocked the door and started the engine. In the confusion, no one paid him any attention. Slowly he drove to the edge of the pavement and stopped.

Brenna emerged from the darkness, Phelan in her arms. She climbed in, yanking her door closed with a resounding thunk. She smelled of smoke and soot.

Both silent, they pulled onto the highway, heading

north. Lights flashing, sirens wailing, two police cars sped past them on the way to the disaster. No doubt this and the fire the night before were the most excitement Hawk's Falls had seen in years.

Leaving the fire behind, Carson finally exhaled. Driving with blind luck, he located another of those deserted dirt roads that appeared to lead to nowhere and turned on it.

Because his hands and arms felt like rubber, he only went a couple of miles before he pulled over on the shoulder and killed the engine.

He looked at Brenna. Wide-eyed, she stared back.

"It's cold," she said, her voice husky.

Was she in shock? Most likely, though the dampness of the chilly night did tend to seep into the bones. He gathered her in his arms, holding her tightly in his lap. Only to keep them both warm. Nothing more. Unable to help himself, he dropped a kiss on the top of her head.

She stiffened. "What was that for?"

Strong emotion rushed him, constricting his chest and clogging his throat. Unprepared, he shook his head and simply tightened his arms around her.

"You could have died." He stared blindly at the top of her head. Brenna, beautiful, bold Brenna, had nearly become an innocent casualty in his quest for justice. He'd failed to protect her, despite his vow to make sure no more lives were lost because of him. The thought of her perishing nauseated him. Made him want to fight something. Someone.

"*We* could have died," she corrected. "But we made it. You, me and Phelan. We're all right."

Avoiding her direct gaze, he reached over the console and gave the puppy a rough pat. Blinking up at him, Phelan licked his hand, then curled into a ball and went to sleep.

Carson felt Brenna shiver in his arms. Delayed shock. He'd been right the first time.

"God, I'm sorry," he said. "I never intended—"

"It wasn't your fault." She sounded so sternly reproving that he couldn't help but smile.

"We were lucky."

He thought of another time, when he hadn't been so lucky. The shot in the back had taken him down. Down and out. He'd nearly died then, but instead had recovered to live with the reality that he'd lost his entire world. Most days since, he'd wished he had died. Only vengeance kept him alive. Only the search for justice kept him going.

After that, he didn't know. Until now, he'd always planned to end it all, to join Becky and Julie in the afterlife.

Now…he wanted to live. Again his own thoughts stunned him. He shied away from the notion, not sure he trusted himself. The very idea seemed foreign. He just didn't know how such a thing could be possible—awakened desires, longing, feelings he'd believed long dead.

Once entirely certain of his own path, now he simply didn't know. All he knew was the soft beauty of the woman he held in his arms. Letting the past go, he buried his face in her hair and breathed in her smoke-tinged scent. Through the soot and ashes, he could still detect the unwavering aroma of flowers clinging to her skin.

"Those Hades' Claws people are nuts," she said.

"Yeah, and dangerous. I tried to warn you." He glanced at his watch. His heart skipped a beat. "We'll never make it to the bus station on time now. I hope Jack gets out okay.''

''Jack! How long—''

''By the time we get there, his bus will have already left.''

''What about the message he's supposed to give you?''

Carson pulled out his cell phone and punched in a number. After the ninth ring, he hung up. ''No answer.''

''Maybe we should go.''

Checking his watch once more, Carson sighed. ''No point.''

His throat still burned. He swallowed, anyway. ''He can call me later. I'm sure he's all right—guys like him know how to survive. He'll call.''

Turning in his arms, she raised her chin. In the dim light of the wintry sun, her skin looked like cream, her eyes huge and dark, her mouth full. Never had she seemed more hauntingly, achingly beautiful. And fragile.

He wanted her safe. Yet she wouldn't let him protect her. ''I'll take you to the bus station if you'll get on the next bus out of here.''

''No.'' Her eyes flashed.

Frustration made his stomach clench. ''Look at what's happened. They won't stop until they kill us. You have to go. I can't let you die because of me.''

''Hey. We're alive.'' Leaning into him, she brushed her lips across his. ''Alive. Go with it. We're all right.''

His heart thudded in his chest. Stunned, he accepted her kiss. She was right. Even now life thickened his blood, stirred his body to readiness. He held himself still, frozen. Alive.

Afraid to breathe, afraid to move. With her mouth she explored his. With sensual slashes of her tongue she tasted. She stroked him, caressed him, teased him. Brought him to an achingly hard readiness, close to losing control.

Adrenaline. It fueled both of them, he knew. In his line of work, such a reaction to a close brush with death was normal. They lived, they breathed. The first rush of shock had left her. With energy still pumping through her veins, Brenna wanted to reaffirm life. With him.

Because he knew better, he fought, but desire and wonder and joy exploded inside him, bubbling up from a long-forgotten place. His pulse pounded. He wanted… He needed… Yet somehow he kept himself utterly and completely still. Under control. Waiting. She touched him, and he surged against her, letting her feel the strength of his desire for her. Her call now, her move.

At his lack of any overt response, she gave a frustrated cry and, completing the turn she had only half started, straddled him. Settling her soft warmth over him with a quiet sigh, she touched him, her small hands everywhere at once, soft and hard, gentle and urgent. Each stroke, each caress, brought him closer and closer to the edge of his iron control.

"Brenna…" He couldn't understand how she, so vibrantly beautiful, could want a broken man like him. That thought, and only that thought, kept him from ripping her clothes off and taking her.

"Carson."

He heard the naked longing in her voice and shuddered. She moved over him, and his body stirred. Her heat seared him through their clothing, wet and warm and willing. His own need escalated—it had been so damn long since he'd felt this way—desire mingling with uncertainty. He closed his eyes, lost in sensation. Inhaling sharply, the scent of smoke from the fire reminded him of things he could not forget.

How he longed to forget. Just once.

He slanted his mouth over hers, hard, demanding. With a glad cry she met him, her passion equal to his, her movements frenzied and urgent.

"Alive," she gasped once more. This time, his heart, his soul, his body, echoed the word.

Alive. Never had he felt more so.

"Brenna." His voice thickened as he gave her a final warning. "Last chance," he said. He knew that if they kept this up, he would take her here, mindless and savage in the front seat of his truck. She deserved better. A soft bed, candlelight, wine.

Turning his head, he attempted to push her away. She resisted, the steering wheel at her back.

"No," she said, and kissed him again.

Finally he surrendered. Lost, he followed where she led. The bleak abyss that had shadowed his days for so long receded, as did the cold, hard leather seat beneath him. He touched her through her clothes, his hands warmed by the heat she radiated. She arched into him, crying out, and with one stroke he felt her come apart under his fingers.

Too much between them—jeans and zippers and sweatshirts. Unnecessary clothing. He wanted silky skin, flesh slick with desire.

As though she'd read his mind, she yanked at his shirt, pulling it over his head and tossing it in the back seat. Caressing his bare skin, she tugged at the edge of his jeans. Guiding her, he helped her find the zipper, helped her pull it down over his swollen body. When she freed him and curled her fingers around his heat, he gasped. So long denied, he surged into her hand, uncontrollable.

"Wait." He grabbed her fingers to keep from embarrassing himself right then and there like an eager adolescent. "I don't have a condom."

She smiled, a slow and sensual thing that held a tinge of sadness. "You haven't, er, been with anyone since—"

"No."

Her kiss took away the sting of that simple word. When she raised her head and met his gaze, she looked solemn. "Then I think we're safe. It's been over a year for me—"

"I'm not a careless man."

Touched, she stroked him again. He moaned and pulled her back for another deep, drugging kiss.

"Enough talking," she growled against his mouth. She arched her back in a long, sensual stretch, head back. One look at her and he lost his battle for control. With her eyes half-closed, she settled over him. Heat. He gave a hoarse cry, struggling for control. She made a sound, then sheathed him deep inside her warmth.

Home. The absurd thought slammed into him with the subtlety of a brick. Brenna. Hot. Wet. Wonderful. *Home.*

How could he ever let her go?

Then he forgot to think, couldn't think, as she began to move.

Chapter 13

How could he sleep? Brenna eyed Carson's form in the uncomfortable passenger seat next to her and shook her head. Inside the vehicle, the night's chill air made the leather seats hard and unforgiving. She shifted, trying to find a comfortable position. Carson apparently had no such problem. Head back, he slept sitting up, a slight smile softening the harsh planes of his face.

Gazing at him, she felt again that softening inside. Longing to glide her fingers over his skin, she clenched her fists to keep from touching him. Instead she watched the even rise and fall of his chest, inhaling the faint musky after-scent of their lovemaking.

Though she had seen many men, both shifters and human, never had she found one as beautiful as Carson. Beautiful. She pondered the word, knowing it was an odd choice to describe a man so hard and wounded. Yet she fancied she saw a new contentment on his face, as though the slaking of his body's hunger for hers had eased a few of his burdens.

Beautiful. Her chest tight, her heartbeat a steady thump in her ears, she envied him his moment of peace.

Sleep was the last thing she wanted. Though sated, she felt energized, charged. Restless, she wanted to run and jump and laugh out loud. Oddly enough, she also wanted to weep. So much had changed between them. They could never go back to the way they had been.

Their lovemaking had been explosive, wild and abandoned. She'd felt like a virgin again. Jeff had been her first and only, yet the one time they'd had sex couldn't hold a candle to this. No one had told her such pleasure was possible. She blushed, feeling a remembered tingling as she contemplated the things she and Carson had done. They hadn't even bothered to remove all their clothing, their passion had been so frenzied.

Yet they'd made love. Carson had possessed her, put an indelible stamp on her soul. It wasn't only the way he'd brought her to her first release. No, they'd forged a bond, a thread that would tie them together now and always.

Always.

The very thought frightened her, even as she exulted in the certainty of it. Things had changed and, hounds help her, she should have known better. Their coming together was everything she'd ever imagined lovemaking could be and more. So much more. Like finally finding the place where she belonged.

A shattering, painful thought, especially since she knew Carson would not want her the same way.

She had to find some distance. She could not allow this to happen again.

Her heart sank. Letting him go would be difficult. How could it not be, when even his masculine scent brought her pleasure? Watching him now, she immediately hungered for more. She desired to touch him, taste the salt of his skin. She wanted to love him again with her body, since he would not accept her soul.

Fool. Though she wanted what had happened between them to be mere lust, nothing stronger, she knew she had given more than her body to Carson. She now felt naked, exposed. Vulnerable.

One final look assured her he still slept deeply. That was good, for if he looked at her, she was afraid he would be able to read the powerful emotion thrumming through her body.

Love. Unable to lie to herself any longer, Brenna admitted the truth. She loved him. With all her heart, all her soul.

Love. Covering her face with her hands, she shifted in the seat and again called herself a fool. There were a thousand reasons why she shouldn't love Carson. He was human and she—she was not. He was broken and bitter and probably incapable of ever loving another woman. Especially one such as she, who could change into a wolf at will. What future could they possibly have together? None.

Yet in her heart of hearts she'd named him her mate. There would be no other for her. Once he had gone, she would remain alone to the end of her days. Alone and childless.

Another thought struck her. Had they made a child together? They'd used no protection. Pregnancy was entirely possible.

Even now, she could be carrying Carson's child. She spread her fingers protectively across her stomach, pondering.

A child. How would Carson react to such a thing? For that matter, what would *she* do?

A child of theirs would be half shifter, half human. She'd heard of such children, though she knew none personally. While the shifter gene was dominant, children born half shifter were not as powerful as full shifters while in their wolf shape. Still, because they had the ability to change, they were accepted unequivocally into the Pack, welcomed and loved like any other cub.

Carson's child. The thought brought a rush of another sort of pleasure. A child of her own. Though her work as a librarian brought her daily human contact, she'd been lonelier than she'd cared to admit.

Her head hurt. Kneading her temples, she gazed out at the black night and felt a primal call. She still needed to change. To slip soundlessly through the woods, unencumbered by human thoughts and emotions.

In the back seat, Phelan stirred, whimpering. He needed a quick trip outside to relieve his bladder. A perfect excuse for her to briefly disappear into the woods to become a wolf.

Quietly, hoping not to disturb Carson, she reached into the back seat and got Phelan. Though at first he wiggled in excitement, a quiet word calmed him. Together they stepped into the night forest.

The woodsy scents of earth and bark and winter

gave her immediate comfort. Phelan bounded ahead, plowing through an occasional snowdrift, tail wagging. Moving more slowly, Brenna followed. She wanted to make certain she was out of sight of the Tahoe before she allowed herself to change.

The moon provided a silvery light, eerie through the leafless trees. Here. Stopping in a small clearing, she turned and lifted her arms to the stars that glittered in the icy sky. Quickly she shed her clothing, making a neat stack next to a large oak.

Power hummed in the crisp air. Finally. A thrill ricocheted through her as she gave way to the craving. Her bones sang as they began to elongate, her heart pumping as she felt the necessary shifting begin to course through her blood. Eventually it would consume her. In a few minutes she would run through the deserted forest, glorying in her full power as a she-wolf. Full-fledged huntress. One of the Pack.

Leaves cracked. Phelan barked, alerting her. Too late, she spun around to face the threat, her energy locked up in the beginnings of the change. Not Carson, but some other man. She saw his shadowy face reflect horror a second before he grabbed her. She tried to fight but, in the middle of changing, with not enough time to complete the process, she was vulnerable, exposed. She had no energy to resist. Nor to complete the change.

Arms clamped around her. He held her, fumbling for something—a weapon. Weakened, she attempted a kick, but it fell far short. Cursing, he tightened his grip. When he covered her face with a sweet-smelling cloth, she tried to bite him. He shoved some of the material in her mouth, gagging her. A sharp taste, metallic and bitter. The rag—some sort of drug. Must.

Not. Breathe. But, inevitably, she had to have air. One gasp to fill her lungs and she felt herself spiraling into oblivion.

Carson jerked awake. Somewhere outside, a dog barked, shrill and furious. Phelan? A quick glance around the Tahoe showed him Brenna had gone, her pet with her.

As he reached for the door handle, he saw headlights coming toward him on the dirt road. Instinctively, he ducked, but not before he saw the front of the van barreling toward him. Ford. Brown. His law-enforcement-trained mind automatically recorded the make and color. The vehicle sped past, bouncing over the rutted road until it vanished from sight.

From deep within the dark forest, Phelan began to howl.

Brenna. Yanking open the door, Carson jumped to the ground and ran.

Here. A tangle of footprints in the snow. Brenna and Phelan and…someone else. A large man. One who wore at least a size thirteen boot.

Phelan barked again, and Carson veered left. Ignoring the nagging pain that blossomed in his side, he headed toward the sound.

Reaching a small clearing where the trampled snow showed signs of a struggle, he cursed. Swiftly he followed the tracks. Abruptly Brenna's footprints ended. Only the stranger's trail led away, followed by Phelan's paw marks.

Brenna. She'd been grabbed. Like Jack had warned, Hades' Claws had come after her. Again moving faster than he'd anticipated, they'd caught him unprepared. Despite Jack's warning, he'd been so sure their next move would be against him.

He hadn't been vigilant. One incident of great sex with Brenna and he'd dropped off to sleep like a man who had a right to. He'd relaxed his guard. Stupid. Now Brenna had been taken. They would kill her if he didn't get to her in time.

Still barking, Phelan rushed into the clearing, straight to Carson. Clearly agitated, the young dog jumped again and again, then ran toward the trees and waited.

Phelan wanted to show him something. Following, Carson went into the trees, surprised to find the road twisted near on the other side. Tire tracks showed where Brenna's abductor had parked.

Carson grabbed his cell phone, hitting redial. Even though Jack should be on the bus, he might know something. Three rings. Four. Still no answer.

On the sixth ring, Jack answered.

"Jack, they've got Brenna."

"Help me." Jack's voice, a full octave higher than normal, sounded terrified. "I missed the bus, and they sent someone here, he's going to—"

Over the phone line, Carson heard the unmistakable sound of a gunshot. Heard Jack's muffled scream, the awful sound of his body as he fell.

"Turner." Another voice—Jack's assailant? "You're too late to help the snitch. He's dead. We've got your girlfriend. She's next."

Then a final click as the man snapped the phone closed.

Forty minutes later, Carson pulled up to the bus station. Three squad cars, lights flashing, blocked the entrance. Yellow police tape fenced in a square near the entrance. Like at the motel fire, a crowd of curious onlookers had gathered.

Carson parked the Tahoe as close as he could. Leaving it running, he crossed to the edge of the crowd, keeping watch for anyone who looked remotely like a biker.

"What's going on?"

A man turned to look at him, his graying, short beard and lined face perplexed. "Man was murdered," he said. "Young guy, too. From the city. Heard he'd just bought a bus ticket to Brooklyn."

Jack. Carson took a deep breath. What about Brenna?

"This man, was he alone?"

"Far as I know." The man peered at Carson. "Why?"

"I knew him. Was he shot?"

"Yes." The man shuffled his feet. His sparkling white sneakers and neatly pressed jeans proclaimed him a tourist.

Carson's cell chirped. "Excuse me." Making his way toward the nearest brick wall, he kept his back against it while he answered.

"Talk to me."

"She's not at the bus station." It was the same voice—Jack's killer.

Carson scanned the crowd. "Is she alive?" He could hardly get the word past the knot in his throat.

"For the time being."

"Are you here?" Carson clenched his fists.

"Nah. Not me." No hesitation in the guttural voice. "If I was, you'd be dead. Like your girlfriend will be soon. Did you know she was naked?" The caller chuckled. "Though the boss made us put her clothes back on."

Swallowing back his rage, Carson kept his voice level. "Where is she? Tell me how to find her."

"Why bother? She's as good as dead."

With a snarl Carson shifted his grip on the phone. "Cut the bull. Let the girl go. I'll offer myself instead. You name the time, the place."

The biker sneered. "A sacrifice?"

"If that's what you want to call it."

"What if we want you both dead?"

"Then I go down shooting. I'll take some of you down with me."

"I'll get back to you." Again that click as the other man disconnected.

Heart hammering, Carson punched the wall. If the man delivered his message, Carson might finally get what he wanted—a face-to-face confrontation with Alex or whoever had killed his family. If he could only work out a way to save Brenna at the same time.

They would never cut a deal, Hades' Claws didn't play by rules. Never had.

Then neither would he. Let them think he was waiting for them to set up a meeting. Meanwhile, he would ditch whoever was watching him and head out to the Hell Hole, figure out a way to get in and rescue Brenna. If he got really lucky, while he was there he would find the SOB who'd ordered her taken and get some answers.

Alex. Brenna's brother. What part did he play in all this? Did he know his own people had taken her? If he did, she ought to be safe. Surely her own brother wouldn't let her come to any harm, or would he?

Carson knew what he would do in Alex's place. If

they'd given him a choice eighteen months ago, he sure as hell would have traded his life for that of his wife and child.

After, when all that he'd lived for had been savagely ripped away from him, he'd longed for death. Prayed for death. Hell, until recently, he still would have welcomed oblivion, once he'd gotten his hands around the murderer's throat. But not anymore.

So many deaths. Because of Carson, Jack had been killed. Now his enemies had Brenna.

No more.

The killing would stop.

Giving the still-gawking crowd one final look, Carson walked away quietly and got in his Tahoe. The battered vehicle creaked and sputtered as he drove slowly away.

He slammed on the brakes as a horrible thought occurred to him. What if Brenna was already dead? What if he was too late to stop them from killing her?

His head began to ache. Since he'd lost his family, he'd lived for the day when he could finally look the bastard who'd killed them in the face. The renegade side of him wanted to pull the trigger himself. The lawman in him voted for arrest and justice.

Even he wasn't a hundred percent certain what he would do when the time came. He just wanted to know.

But not at the risk of yet another life.

He wiped his hand across his mouth, unsurprised to find it was shaking. After being focused on one goal for so long, his grip on reality had been disturbed. He no longer recognized facts or lies, reality or fantasy.

But one thing he did know—Brenna Lupe was special. She'd crept into his heart and stayed there. He wouldn't be too late to save her. Fate couldn't be so cruel. Brenna was the one person he wholeheartedly believed in since he'd lost his entire family. She was good and innocent and blameless. He would stake his life on it. Now he might have to.

Determined, he pressed the gas pedal to the floor and headed north, toward the Hell Hole.

Brenna woke in a dark room. She came awake fighting. Sucking in great gulps of air, she attempted to ward off an absent enemy. Her fists came up short, unable to move. Any attempt at movement brought sharp pain.

A look at her wrists showed her why. She'd been handcuffed, one hand to each side of a headboard.

Shaking her head, she blinked furiously, trying to clear her sight. The room appeared to be shrouded in fog. She swallowed, grimacing at the metallic taste. The objects in the darkened room receded, came closer, then danced away. Blurry. No sharp edges. Her heartbeat felt sluggish, her limbs heavy.

Finally she understood why. She'd been drugged. One of the worst possible things that could happen to a shape-shifter. If she lost control of her body's ability to change, she could mix the molecules. The end result could be death or worse, a horrific maddened creature out of mankind's worst nightmares.

Deliberately she calmed herself, using relaxation techniques to focus. She'd always prided herself on her control; she would call on that ability now to aid her.

The dark room didn't bother her; like others of her kind, smell was her dominant sense, enabling her to see in a way her eyes did not. She sniffed, groaning aloud. Whatever drug she'd been given had dulled even that important faculty.

Still, though unable to probe deeply, she was able to detect the first layer of scents. The room smelled musty, as though it had been unused and closed up for a long time. The clogging scents of dust and decay made her sneeze.

Next she attempted to listen, blocking out the sound of her own heartbeat and labored breathing, trying to hear voices, a radio, some conversation—anything to give her a clue as to where she might be.

She heard only silence. Felt only confusion.

She could not change to save herself. All she could hope was that Alex would learn of her capture. Once her brother knew Hades' Claws had taken her, she would be safe.

She hoped.

With a groan, she swallowed. She hated that now even she doubted her own brother's intentions, thanks to the way he'd behaved around Carson.

Carson. A fresh wave of emotion swamped her. Would he look for her? She didn't want to put him in danger because of her own foolishness. Bottom line: she would rather her life be at risk than his.

She loved the man.

Her eyes filled with tears. The drug? Or her own burgeoning sensitivity? She sighed. What a time to fall deeply, hopelessly in love with a human.

At least, she thought, she could find some humor in this horrific mess. Things couldn't get any worse. Or could they? She remembered a similar thought she'd shared with Carson the day before. The room had blown up then.

Yes, things could certainly get worse. She had to find a way out. Closing her eyes, she ignored the pitch and roll of the floor, knowing it was the drug wreaking havoc with her senses. She must regain control. She needed to come up with a plan. She had to figure a way out.

Carson didn't stop to plan, or even to think. This time he couldn't lose, couldn't afford to fail. To rescue Brenna, he would have to act solely on gut instinct and impulse. He had to get her out—now. No time to waste. He'd delayed in getting to Jack, and now Jack was dead. He wouldn't make the same mistake again—not with Brenna's life at stake.

Once he reached the Hell Hole, he drove past and parked off the road, near a copse of leafless trees, even though the dark night hid the car well enough.

Leaving a protesting Phelan in the truck, he slipped on his black work jacket, thankful the bright yellow DEA logo was emblazoned only on the back, and began to walk toward the gate, taking care to stay near the trees in case he needed to take cover.

No cars disturbed the late-night peace. The faint moonlight turned snowdrifts silver, bathing the trees in a ghostly luminescence. Yet danger lurked here, in the depth of the dark forest, in the compound where evil slept.

There had to be a way in. Encircled by the odd fence, the perimeter of the Hell Hole was clearly marked. He studied the stonework, looking for a break. There, where the wall made a slight turn—one place looked less intimidating than the rest. At roughly four feet tall, some of the rock had crumbled, leaving a gap. This low point would be his best bet in scaling the glass-shard protected fence.

Ice in the breeze made him shiver. The end of his long journey waited inside these walls.

Focus. Center. One thing at a time.

First—get inside, find Brenna and get her out.

Once she was safe, then he would hunt down his former partner and settle things once and for all.

He placed his hand on the stone, feeling the cold seep into him. Focus.

How to breach their security and remain undetected?

When a survey of the surrounding trees failed to reveal any other security cameras besides the ones aimed directly at the gate, he let out breath he hadn't even realized he'd been holding. Despite what he'd told Brenna on their trip out here earlier, he doubted the woods were filled with motion sensors. It would make a lot more sense to outfit the fence itself with an alarm rather than try to monitor the entire forest. Half-assed security, but still more than enough for an ordinary home.

This place was far from normal. He was pinning his hopes on the fact that Hades' Claws wouldn't believe anyone would be foolish enough to invade their headquarters. He hoped to use that arrogance against them now.

Limited planning session finished, he backed up. He took the low point of the fence at a dead run. Vaulting over, he made it with only one shard of jagged glass stabbing his palm. The cut bled, but he ignored it and stood still, heartbeat a loud thumping in his ears.

No alarms sounded; no spotlights began to sweep

the woods. All remained quiet and still. He'd been right, then—they only monitored the gate. Apparently he hadn't triggered the sensors. So far, so good.

Slipping from tree to tree, just in case they posted guards, he finally saw the house through the tangled branches. Still a good fifty yards off, the low-slung ranch was an architectural holdover from the fifties. Unpainted and slightly weathered, the structure hid behind overgrown shrubbery. This had the singular result of making the place appear to blend with the forest, especially with all of the windows dark, as they were now. In the silver moonlight, the cedar siding appeared to glow. Overall, Carson found the effect eerie rather than truly menacing. But he, more than anyone, knew better than to trust simple appearances. Nothing was ever what it seemed. If he were to trip an alarm, he had no doubt that bikers would swarm over the yard, armed to the teeth.

He crept closer. There had to be a way inside without alerting any of the occupants. His next step would be figuring out where they were keeping Brenna.

Moving silently, he made his way around to the side of the house. Checking his watch, he stumbled. Caught himself. Nearly midnight. He took a deep breath, blew it out in a frosted plume. His nerves jangled. With an effort, he steadied them. Years of undercover work had taught him to trust his gut reactions—and his gut said something was off-kilter. There was something…wrong about the situation.

He took inventory. Midnight. Dark woods. Even darker house. Too quiet. No dogs. He found it hard to believe a bunch of bikers went to bed so early. Unless they were expecting him, he couldn't imagine them sitting around in the darkened house.

Unless they were gone.

He froze, unable to consider that possibility. If they were gone, they'd taken Brenna elsewhere. He would have a hell of a time trying to find her.

As he stared at the house, a light blinked on, spilling bright yellow light into the backyard. No blinds or curtains shaded the window. Ducking behind a thick oak, Carson watched a large man enter the room, bending over as he fiddled with something out of Carson's line of sight. Carson moved forward.

A leaf crackled. He spun. Too late.

Chapter 14

A loud crash came from the hall. Startled into wakefulness, Brenna attempted to sit up, yelping in pain as the handcuffs yanked her back to the bed. Footsteps pounded. She heard a thump, a curse, another crash, sounds of a scuffle.

Two men, maybe three, fighting. Were there guards outside her door? Straining to hear, she went very still. She heard a low voice give a guttural order but could not make out the words. The walls shook from another huge thump. She heard grunts and the horrible resonance of fists connecting. Finally there was an ominous-sounding thud, followed by silence. Then she heard only the steady drum of her own heartbeat in her ears.

Her door squeaked open. The light clicked on again. Blinking against the sudden blinding brightness, she squinted at the man standing in the doorway. Shorty, the sour-smelling man who earlier had brought her food, grinned at her before disappearing briefly. When he returned, he backed into the room, dragging an unconscious body under the arms. Though his head was turned, she recognized the black DEA jacket and matching cap. Her heart stuttered, began to thud erratically. Carson. They had Carson. His hands had been cuffed in front of him.

After depositing Carson in an unceremonious heap on the floor next to the bed, Shorty produced one more pair of steel handcuffs. They were twins to the ones he'd used to shackle Brenna to the bed. Since her feet were free, Shorty yanked Carson's leg up and cuffed his ankle to hers. The cold steel bit into her flesh.

"Too tight?" Leering at her, her captor shook his head, grinning.

"Yes," she said. "Too tight. And you've got him upside down."

"Tough," Shorty sneered. "He can try and fix that when he wakes up. Hell, he ought to thank me. Now you two can be together. Die with each other, too, most likely. Nemo should give me a big bonus for this one."

He aimed his steel-toed boot and kicked Carson, catching him hard in the leg. Semiconscious, Carson gave a muffled groan.

It took every ounce of willpower she had to keep herself from baring her teeth and lunging forward. Only fear of her inability to control the change kept Brenna motionless. Until she was certain the drugs had left her system, she dared not risk it.

"He's gonna wish he'd died the first time, along with his wife and kiddo." With a laugh, Shorty leaned in to chuck her under the chin. Brenna growled low in her throat, baring her teeth at him. Immediately she felt the change begin in her. Horrified, she clamped down, closing her mouth.

"Hey, girl, I like 'em feisty," Shorty said, ruffling her hair as an added insult. Still chuckling, he waved a set of keys at her. "Too bad you can't reach 'em." Dropping them with a clank on the dresser, he left the room, slamming the door closed behind him.

Brenna calmed herself. She took an analytical inventory of her system. The room no longer danced and swam through a blur. She could once more see angles and corners. Though her mouth felt as if it had been stuffed with cotton, she no longer tasted metal. Lifting her head, she tried to scent the air. This time she could detect the faint odors of perspiration and blood.

Carson. Tied as she was, she couldn't help him. He lay on his back on the floor, the leg that had been shackled to hers pulling at her like a dead weight. Hounds help her if he tried to roll over.

"Carson," she said softly. No response. She wiggled, propping her back against the headboard, trying to ease the blood flow to her hands and now her leg.

"Carson." She tried again. She had to wake him before he moved and stretched her between him and the bed like some medieval torture rack. Then it would be a simple matter of making sure the drugs were gone. She would change, the cuffs would drop off, and they would be free.

But what about Carson. If she changed, would he despise her? Vividly remembering how Jeff, the man who'd asked her to marry him, had reacted to the truth about her nature, she knew the last thing she wanted was for Carson to find out.

Jeff's reaction had killed him.

For years, Brenna hadn't been able to rid herself of the idea that he'd chosen death rather than a life with someone such as her. Ridiculous, she knew now, especially since his death had been a horrible accident, but it had happened because in his shock and horror he had run from her to his car. Reckless driving, fueled by confusion and shock, had caused him to have a head-on collision with a gasoline tanker truck. Both Jeff and the truck driver had been burned beyond recognition.

No, she really didn't want Carson to find out she was a shape-shifter. But if she didn't change, they would both be trapped and die. Unless her brother suddenly appeared with the handcuff keys and released them, she had no choice.

Carson attempted to move his leg, yanking hard at hers. She yelped.

"Brenna?" He went still. Raising his head and licking the blood off his cracked lips, he pushed himself up on his elbows. Blanching, he took in the situation with a quick glance. "Damn."

"Hey," she said softly. "How badly are you hurt?" His face had been bruised and his lip split open, but even battered, she still found him beautiful. She wanted to reach out and smooth the hair from his forehead, but she couldn't.

"Not bad." He attempted to shift his weight, wincing at the pain. "They hit me from behind. Once again, I screwed up."

"Me too." She had no answer for him, no words to soothe the tortured self-reproach she saw in his eyes. She blamed herself enough for both of them. She had powers ordinary humans did not. Of the two of them, she should have been the most able to evade capture. Like Carson, she'd been taken by surprise.

Even the mere thought of changing made her body resonate with need. With every heartbeat, every inhalation of breath, the desire sharpened, unbearably intense.

But she had to make sure the drugs had worn off before she gave in to the urge. If some other way out presented itself, she would take it. She would only change as a last resort.

"My leg—" Struggling to rise without yanking her apart, Carson pushed himself closer to the bed. Twisting, he managed to get his knee under him, propelling himself against the side of the bed. Since his hands were cuffed, he could only use them for leverage to thrust himself up.

"Help me." He raised his head, dark gaze meeting hers. "I can't hold this position long—hurts like hell. When I come up this time, hold your leg still. I'll have to use you as a sort of anchor, but I think I can make it up there."

Swallowing, she nodded.

With a grunt, he pushed and twisted at the same time. Clearing the edge of the mattress, he landed with his chin squarely on her groin.

She froze.

"Sorry," he said, his gaze darkening. With a neat motion, he rolled to the side. That meant she had to scoot over as far right as her handcuffed wrists would allow.

"Thanks," he muttered, attempting to wiggle into the space between her and the edge with minimal contact between him. But even if he lay on his side, with his left ankle chained to her right one, it wasn't possible. With that leg underneath him, they still had to mingle ankles. He looked like a bruised human pretzel.

"This isn't going to work." His words echoed her own thoughts. She looked at him, the beginnings of desire subjugated by the ever-present urge to change, and swallowed. "You'll have to lie on my other side, partially on top of me," she said.

He narrowed his eyes. "It's the only way, huh?" he said.

"Yes."

"I'll try not to hurt you." With an awkward twist and roll, he settled his weight over her, the hard length of his body pressing against hers for an instant. He jockeyed to find a comfortable spot. Her body heat increased, making her feel as though she were burning.

"There." He sighed. Closing his eyes, he sagged against her.

"Carson? We've got to get out of here. Carson?"

He didn't answer. The dead weight of him told her that he was unconscious.

She eyed the handcuff keys on the dresser. A mere twelve feet away. So close, but out of reach. Even if she extended her leg and Carson stretched out to his full length, they couldn't reach them.

A window sat midway along the other wall. It was reachable, though only by Carson, and only if they did some contorting.

There had to be a way to escape. Had to be.

But the only way she could think of involved her changing.

Several hours later she shifted for the twentieth time. Her hands were asleep again, the painful pins-

and-needles making her grit her teeth as she forced herself to do finger and wrist exercises.

Dim light streamed in through the blinds. Dawn. Her bladder was full, though she'd only had a small sip of the lukewarm water Shorty had offered the night before.

Carson shifted his weight with her, though this time the movement caused a perceptible change in his breathing. She took a deep breath and drank in the sight of him. With his face inches away from hers on the pillow, she longed to plant featherlight kisses on the dusky beginnings of a beard on his unshaven cheeks, but she dared not. He would awaken soon. Once he did, he would be in no small amount of pain, but at least he was alive.

That had to count for something.

She couldn't watch him die. Testing her own reflexes, she felt a noticeable improvement. Even if he despised her after, she would change if she had to in order to save his life. Heck, if they didn't let her go to the rest room soon, she would change just so she could relieve her bladder.

From out in the other part of the house, she heard the early-morning noises of people stirring, the clang of a skillet, the sound of the pipes as water ran. At the faint aroma of brewing coffee, her mouth began to water.

From the hall came another sound, this time the uneven thudding of a man running. Outside her closed door, two men talked in low voices that she strained to hear but could not. The back of her neck began to tingle.

Something was up. She sensed urgency in the very

air, in the faintly acrid scents of their captors' perspiration.

Danger. Excitement. Those emotions rolled off the
men in the house, reaching her in waves.

"Brenna?" Raising his head, Carson sounded the
way he looked. "Damn. I feel like I've been run over
by a freight train."

This time she couldn't resist—she reached out and
gently kissed his cracked lips. He went utterly still.

"They worked you over." She kept all traces of
emotion out of her voice.

"Yeah." He laughed, though his laugh sounded
more like a choked-off cough. "Hurts like hell."

She studied him. "Why'd you wear the jacket?"

With a shrug, he grimaced. "It's black, it's warm.
I didn't intend to get captured."

In the hall, a man shouted. They could hear the
words "Out front!" More footsteps ran past.

Carson pushed himself to a sitting position.
"What's going on?"

Listening intently, she shook her head. "Something. I don't know what."

He glanced at his watch and swore. "What day is
this?"

She had to think. "Thursday." Still, she strained
to hear. The house seemed to be enveloped in chaos—
men shouting orders and running.

"The drug deal. If we stretch, can we reach the
window?"

She stared at him blankly. "Why? If they start
shooting out there, the window won't be safe."

"I don't care."

Of course he didn't. Maybe the edginess in his tone
decided her, or perhaps the sudden hardness she saw

in his gaze. Either way, Brenna knew what mattered to Carson above all else was his thirst for justice, for revenge.

"I need to see outside and find out what's going on."

"It's on the west side of the house. Can you see the front from there?"

His face full of impatience, he grimaced. "I won't know until I try."

Hating her feeling of helplessness, she wanted to growl her frustration. Sometimes being a wolf was much easier.

"If you think it'll work, let's try." With a curt nod to indicate her agreement, she motioned for him to attempt to push away. He rolled, their legs still cuffed together, pushing himself to his knees. Shuffling, crawling, he made it to the edge of the bed, leaning on the windowsill for support.

The metallic handcuffs bit into the skin of her wrists. Pain. Out of nowhere, the urge to change ripped through her. This time she found it even more difficult to push away.

"Not yet," she said under her breath.

"What?" Carson shot her an impatient glance.

"Nothing." Gesturing at the window with her chin, she forced an impersonal smile. "You wanted to see if you could see out the window. Have at it."

As she spoke, she heard more shouts. She smelled a faint hint of smoke. Fire? She quelled a rising sense of panic. No wolf—or human, for that matter—could endure for too long the threat of being trapped in a fire. Every sense on the alert, she listened. But she heard no roaring or crackle of flames, nor felt any hint of the searing heat that such a blaze wrought. They had time. She prayed she was right.

Peering out the blinds, Carson looked so long without speaking that Brenna couldn't resist giving the leg handcuffed to his a quick jerk.

"Patience." He kept his attention focused on the window.

This time a quiet growl escaped her. He didn't appear to notice.

"The hell with patience." Though her hands were numb from the bite of the handcuffs, her arms were aching again. Her shoulders and neck felt as if she'd been stretched on a medieval rack. "Tell me what's going on."

"A black stretch limo with full biker escort just pulled up outside. Looks like Jack was right—something more than a drug deal is going to happen today."

More footsteps and voices out in the hall. The guard outside their door shouted good-natured greetings to the others.

Carson spoke again. "A bunch of the gang just went outside to greet the limo."

"Alex?" She let her worry show in her voice.

"He's there. Front and center." Carson gave her a layered look. "Has your brother been to see you since you were captured?"

"Of course not." Though she started off strong, her voice faltered. "He doesn't know I'm here."

"You're certain?"

She heard disbelief in his husky voice.

"Of course I am." Her sharp tone dared him to doubt. "If he knew, I wouldn't be cuffed to a bed. And you."

"Are those the keys?"

"Yes."

"I want to see if I can get to them."

"There's no way we can reach that far." She grimaced. "This hurts enough as it is."

His gaze raked her stretched-out body. "If you can make it a little longer, I'd like to see what else happens out front."

"I'm fine," she said. "But I smell smoke and it's getting worse. With all of them focused on that limo, this would be a good time to escape."

Now she had his full attention.

He cocked his head. "Any plans?"

The hell with it. Maybe changing now wouldn't be such a bad idea. She gave him a measuring look. He'd already turned back toward the window.

"I wonder if the DEA is here."

No sooner had he spoken than she heard a rapid staccato of sound from outside.

She tensed. "What the—"

"Gunshots," Carson said. He swore. "The guys in the suits were barely out of the limo. Looks like some trigger-happy idiot jumped the gun."

"Alex." Worried for her brother, her first thought was to escape the cuffs. Once she changed, they would slip right off a wolf's slender paws. Instinctively, she began the process.

"Brenna." Carson's sharp voice brought her back. Tamping down her impatience, she hastily rearranged herself internally.

"What?" Taking deep gulps of smoke-tinged air, she looked at him. Something in the craggy lines of his face made her pulse skip a beat.

"Alex?" she asked, her voice tight. "Please tell me Alex is okay."

"He's fine." Now he left the window and crawled over in front of her. "Stay calm."

Heart in her throat, she nodded.

"The building is on fire," he said.

"I thought so." Animal instinct—flight or fight—filled her. "Carson, I—" She needed to change. Now.

"Take it easy," he said. "Rest your arms. If we're going to figure out a way out of this, you can't panic."

Right. She couldn't afford to panic. Especially if there were still drugs floating around in her blood. "I'm fine." Lifting her chin, she swallowed. "I don't like being helpless, that's all."

"None of us do." He moved his leg, rattling the set of cuffs that linked them together. "These are too tight."

She smiled at that. "Yeah. At least you can move your hands." Then, sobering, she tugged at her arms, cuffed tightly to the sturdy wooden post of the bed.

It was time. She would give him a warning first.

"Look," she said. "I'm going to do something now to free us. Don't freak out on me, okay?"

Disbelief and hope warred in his dark gaze.

She closed her eyes and summoned her strength, ready to begin.

Change.

Outside, chaos sounded. There were more sharp cracks of gunfire, more shouts and running. The scent of smoke grew stronger. The air seemed to thicken, heavy and acrid. Again she fought to ignore the interruption, using all her strength to cleanse her blood, to start the change.

Carson touched her arm, causing her to jump. She opened her eyes and glared at him.

"What?"

"If you're going to do something, do it now. The fire's getting closer."

"I know." She glared at him. Her eyes stung; her throat was clogged. Each breath burned her lungs. Air—she couldn't seem to breathe.

Panic and instinct warred within her. Though she needed more time to check herself for drugs, she didn't have it.

"When they bombed the motel, we made it," Carson reminded her. "We'll get out somehow."

Somehow? They hadn't been chained to the bed in the motel room. Well, she would soon take care of that.

"I'm sorry," she gasped, feeling the tremors begin as her cells started to shift. She yanked again at the metal that cuffed her to the bed, a futile, final attempt to set a miracle in motion.

But the handcuffs held.

The smoke became a weapon, bludgeoning them. Fire lapped at the door, tendrils of flame seeking entrance, crackling, hissing.

Change.

Her heartbeat raced. Though the altering of her body had her swaying, still she saw the orange glow of flames, felt the heat, tasted the bitter tang of smoke. Carson's craggy face swam before her, his eyes dark with the sickening belief that this was how it would end. He thought they would die here, like trapped animals tethered in a burning barn. With every fiber, every nerve ending in her, Brenna felt savage joy that her changing would prevent that from happening.

Human. Wolf. Wholly in the grip of the change, she welcomed her animal nature, hastening the sudden shifting of molecules and cells. As her limbs elongated, narrowed, she felt the useless handcuffs slide from her bones, clattering to the floor.

Ferocious fierce strength—*wolf!*

By her actions, Carson, too, was freed, his handcuffs dangling from one ankle, useless. They could reach the keys now and free him. And because of her changing, he would finally know what she was, what she could become.

She couldn't resist, even in her lupine form, glancing once at the man she loved above all others, even though she knew if she saw horror and repulsion on his face, the pain would sear her heart as badly as a fiery death.

Their eyes—man and wolf, Brenna and Carson—met and held. In his gaze she saw disbelief. Shock. But he reached out his hand, and she felt him thread his fingers through her furry pelt. Wonder and joy exploded in her. Hope. Yearning.

Though doing so now was extremely dangerous, in an instant she changed back to Brenna, human woman. She stepped into her torn clothes, then unlocked the cuffs. Grabbing his outstretched hand in hers, she clutched him tightly. Then, through flame and smoke she led him outside the burning house to safety.

Had they given him hallucinogenic drugs? Rubbing his eyes furiously, Carson blinked through the heavy smoke as he fumbled to unlock the handcuffs from his wrists. He had to be on some sort of drug, because he could have sworn he'd just seen Brenna shimmer and somehow become a huge silver wolf. The hand-cuffs had slipped off, freeing them both.

She'd been a wolf. A huge, beautiful, silver wolf. Snarling. For an instant, then... He rubbed his eyes, glancing at her again. Had to be drugs. Had to be. Because after somehow slipping the cuffs, Brenna stood right next to him, her hand clutching his. Not a wolf at all. Beautiful, yes, and courageous, but human. Brenna.

"Did you..." he started to ask. But she held up her hand and shook her head, a slight smile playing across her full lips.

"Not now," she said. "We've got to find Alex."

Alex. Though she'd seemed to know what he'd been about to ask and hadn't denied it, she was right. Even though they both had different reasons, they needed to find her brother.

Still...

"I thought I saw—"

Ignoring him, Brenna started moving, tugging him along after her. He had to hurry to catch up. Side by side they crossed to the front of the burning building. Even though the gunshots had died down, he felt a moment's apprehension. The protective instinct so deeply ingrained in him told him they should take cover. But with Brenna striding boldly forward, the best he could do would be to hope to shield her. So he didn't bother to conceal himself, aware that he, with the bright-yellow DEA emblazoned on the back of his jacket, would be an easier target than she. At the slightest hint of gunfire, he would knock her to the ground.

But, oblivious to the danger, she marched forward. Fiercely intent, she continued to search, ignoring the men milling around them, some of them in custody, cuffed and bleeding, ignoring, too, the others who were down for the final count. She cared only for one thing, had only one purpose, one goal. To find Alex.

Carson grabbed a gun from a fallen guard and went after her.

A man ran past them, head down. Two others came from the side of the burning building and tackled and cuffed him. They led the man away without paying Brenna and Carson any mind. His DEA jacket, no doubt.

Again gunfire erupted. On the other side of the house another shoot-out was going on. Still she pressed forward.

Things looked about over—after that first wild shot, the Feds had swooped in. Watching Brenna's back for threats, Carson counted no less than three different agencies among the milling men of the invading army: DEA, FBI, ATF. In an odd sort of irony, his own DEA jacket was keeping him safe from his own agency, many of whom didn't recognize him, though he knew they would drag his ass in for questions when this was all over. Should he still be standing.

But he wasn't focused on that right now. He had to protect Brenna from her own brother. Alex had been willing to sacrifice his own sister for greed. Carson had to be there for the woman he loved when she finally realized what kind of man her twin had become.

The woman he loved. Once before, Alex had taken his family from him. Carson would kill him or die before he let anything happen to Brenna.

That revelation should have shocked him, especially since he didn't know if she really had changed into something decidedly not human.

Drugs? Or reality?

It didn't matter. Whatever she might be, she was still his Brenna. *His.* For now, for this exact nanosecond in time, he would focus every breath, every heartbeat, every fiber of his being on protecting her, especially once they found his enemy. After Brenna saw what Alex had become, he was going down.

Edging around a corner, Carson finally sighted his target. *Target.* Yeah, that was how he'd come to think of this man who'd once been his partner. An inanimate object—not a person.

Alex saw him at the same instant. Narrowed his eyes at the sight of his sister, who remained at Carson's side.

Carson raised his gun.

Alex raised his, too.

Target in sights. Still, Carson's fingers merely hovered over the trigger. One squeeze, one shot to the chest, and the big man would die.

Beside him, Brenna gave a stifled cry, a gasp.

God help him, this was her brother, her blood. Carson couldn't help remembering Alex as his partner, his best friend.

This was Alex. *Alex.*

While Carson hesitated, Alex did not. He fired.

Chapter 15

Carson jerked, but the bullet went wild. From behind him, someone grunted. Another man. Whirling, Carson saw Brenna leap forward at the exact instant the other guy squeezed off a shot. She knocked away the gun, but the bullet went—where? Brenna reared back. She spun and dropped to her knees. Head down, she gave a muffled cry.

No time to think. Carson raised his gun and shot. The man fell, crimson blossoming on his shirt. Pivoting, Carson brought his weapon to bear on Alex.

"Brenna?" Keeping Alex dead center, Carson backed over to her. Hunkered down. "Are you all right?"

Her hair a dark curtain shielding her face, she raised her head and grimaced, showing white teeth. The orange glow of the flames reflected in her brown eyes. "I'm fine." She sounded winded.

He didn't believe her.

His gun arm wobbled. Steadying it, he kept his weapon on Alex while he pushed away her hands from her shoulder. Scarlet stained her sweatshirt.

"You've been shot." His gut clenched.

"Let me see."

She moved away. "Alex," she said. "He saved your life."

"No. You saved my life. We need to get you to an ambulance."

"Alex fired first," she insisted. "He didn't shoot at you. He hit that guy in the stomach. Kept you from taking a bullet in the back."

She was right, Carson realized. "Why?" He stared at his former friend, now nemesis.

Stone-faced, Alex lowered his gun. "He was gonna shoot you." His grim expression showed his awareness that Carson still had a weapon trained on him. Dead center, finger on the trigger. Then he looked past Carson to his sister, concern softening the harsh planes of his face.

"Are you all right, Bren?"

Nodding, she pushed herself to her feet. "I'll live." She kept both hands pressed against her shoulder. "You know me. I heal fast."

Carson sucked in his breath.

"He saved your life," she repeated, raising her voice to be heard over the roar and crackle of the flames. "He could have killed you, but he didn't."

"I realize that." While he'd hesitated, Alex could have taken him down with one shot. Instead he'd fired to save Carson's life, even though he knew Carson wanted to blow him away.

None of it made sense. Unless...

Part of the building went down. A side wall crum-

bled, giving way to the fire's fury. A man ran scream-
ing from the inferno, his entire body on fire. Two
others tackled him, knocking him to the ground and
rolling.

Carson focused on Alex. "Tell me the truth. Why
not shoot me when you know I plan to bring you in?"

At his words, Brenna shifted. "Bring him in?"

"I couldn't kill him." He met her eyes. "Once,
maybe, I would have. Now, because he's your
brother, because you love him, I'm going to arrest
him and bring him in to stand trial."

Shouts came from the other side of the burning
house as the roof collapsed. Flames roared into the
sky, sending smoke and sparks over them in a shower.

"You're right, Carson. I didn't save your life,"
Alex kept his hands at his sides. "Not this time. My
shot didn't take him down. Brenna saved your life.
She stepped between you and his gun."

"So your shot," Carson heard his voice go flat,
"was only to protect your sister."

Alex shook his shaggy head. "And you, idiot. Put
the gun down." He took a step forward, holding his
own weapon loosely, hand at his side.

Carson ignored him. "Freeze. Alex Lupe, you're
under arrest for the murders of Becky Turner and Julie Turner. You have the right to remain silent. You
have the—"

"Stop." Alex held up his hand, his expression tortured. "I didn't kill Julie and Becky, Carson. I was
too late to save them, but I tried. Damn it, they were
like my family, too. I loved them. You have to know
that. You saw me with a gun, maybe you even saw
me shoot, but you didn't see who I shot. That day, I
did save your life."

Confused and exhausted, Carson swayed on his feet, though he didn't change his position. Weapon on target. Finger near the trigger.

Beside him, Brenna made a strangled sound. She sank to her knees. Carson's heart stopped.

Brenna or Alex? If he had to make a choice, he chose Brenna.

He lowered the pistol. And went to her.

"Let me see." Tenderly he swept back the hair from her face. Capturing her hands, he moved them so he could see her wound again.

"I'm fine," she protested, pushing him away. "Alex—"

All around them, smoke and fire and noise. Men down, men being led away in handcuffs. The acrid, coppery smell of gunpowder, of ashes and fire. The flash of cameras. Reporters already? No. The crime scene guys took photos.

Occupied in fighting the blaze and rounding up stragglers, a few of the federal agents glanced their way and moved on. No one interrupted them, seeing only a fellow agent in their matching, standard-issue jacket as he talked to two others.

Alex took another step forward. "Your cover was blown. We're not sure exactly how or by whom. I heard about the hit and went after the guy. I thought I could get there in time to stop it." The lines in Alex's face reflected his own pain.

"Instead I was too late. But I got there in time to take down the shooter before he finished the job. That's what you saw. I shot the guy who'd just shot you in the back. Stopped him from putting another bullet in you."

Carson stared at him blankly, cradling Brenna in

his arms. She watched his face silently, hope and love mingled with the pain he saw in her expressive eyes.

Carson shook his head, trying to think.

"Don't you remember me calling your name?" Alex came closer. "I ordered you to hang on."

"No." He searched the other man's face. "After I saw you throw away the gun, I don't remember anything until I woke in the hospital room. I never saw anyone else. Just you."

"The DEA knew there was another guy. The shooter. The guy I killed. They couldn't reveal that and risk blowing my cover. So they put the story out that I did it as some sort of initiation test."

"You didn't kill them," Carson said slowly, woodenly. "But Hades' Claws believed you did."

Immobile, Alex jerked his head in a quick nod. "I had to stay inside to find out who'd ordered the hit. I also had to excuse my dropping the guy they'd sent to do it, so I said you shot him. Since he was dead and couldn't tell, the story worked."

"I used to wish I'd died, too."

The corners of Alex's mouth twitched. "What, and miss all this?"

"I thought it was you. I've been hunting the wrong man all along. I want the name of the murdering bastard. The guy who ordered them killed."

"We got him. His game's over."

Holding himself still, Carson tensed. Chest tight, he waited to hear the true name of the man he'd been seeking for so long. Then he felt Brenna's hand on his shoulder, comforting. With only her touch, she kept him sane.

Carson kissed the top of her head. He looked at Alex.

"Senator Guiley. Top dog. We've got him in custody."

"The guy in the limo."

Alex nodded. "New York State Senator and drug lord. He raked in millions. What was one agent's family to him? He ordered the hit. He wanted you dead."

With a sound of disgust, Carson looked away. "All this time," he muttered, scarcely able to take it all in. "All this friggin' time."

He buried his head in Brenna's hair, inhaling deeply. His eyes full, he breathed in her beloved scent. Despite the fire and the smoke, she still smelled like spring.

Brenna—his rock, his love. Head bowed, he struggled to regain control of his emotions.

"I'm sorry," Alex said.

Unable to speak, Carson swallowed. When he finally lifted his head, he saw the man who'd meant to kill him lying on the ground, blood drying on his shirt.

Brenna sagged in his arms.

"She's unconscious." He heard panic in his voice. He pushed back her shirt at the shoulder, gently lifting the blood-soaked material from her skin.

Alex clapped a hand on his shoulder. "It doesn't look deep. I think his shot winged her." He swallowed, visibly shaken. "But you got him in time."

"We need to get the paramedics over. I want her thoroughly checked."

"She'll be all right. She's not badly hurt."

Carson narrowed his eyes. "How do you know that?"

"She's my twin," Alex said simply. "I know."

For the first time it occurred to Carson to ask about

what he'd thought he'd seen earlier, when Brenna had slipped the handcuffs. But, he thought as he studied the other man, if Brenna could change into a wolf, Alex was capable of the same thing.

His head throbbing, Carson decided to ask. "I—"

Like his sister, Alex seemed to know instinctively what Carson had been about to say. "Not now."

Two federal agents charged around the corner, guns drawn, too late. They skidded to a halt, backing off when Alex waved them away.

"You know they'll want to debrief you."

"Later. I've got to talk to Brenna."

Alex's gaze sharpened. "What do you want with her?"

"My entire future."

"Really?" Alex's voice seemed unnecessarily curt. The steely glint in his dark eyes carried a warning.

"Damned if I'm going to ask your permission."

"He saw me change." Brenna lifted her head, her voice weak.

Alex frowned. "When?"

"To get free of the handcuffs."

Carson kept his arms around her. "You mean when you—"

"Became a wolf. Yes."

"How?"

Alex ignored the question. "Among our people, it is forbidden to change in front of a human."

"You're worried because she broke some stupid rule?" Clenching his jaw, Carson inhaled. "We were handcuffed to the bed. The building was on fire. She did it to free us. She saved both our lives."

"I won't let you hurt her. She's my sister. I love her."

"I do, too." Lowering his gaze, Carson looked at Brenna as he spoke. Her eyes filled with tears. "I love you."

She sat up, grimacing as the movement caused her pain. "Even though you know what I am?"

Carson hesitated. As an undercover agent, he'd thought he'd seen it all. Now he realized he'd barely scratched the surface.

"What are you?"

"We're shape-shifters." Brenna's low voice was edgy, yet controlled. "We're an ancient race."

"Werewolves."

"In a way." Alex shrugged. "Though we rarely howl at the moon. And we can control it, for the most part. We aren't compelled to change because of a full moon or anything like that. We try to integrate ourselves into society and live normal lives among humans. Insiders know us as the Pack."

Carson turned to Brenna. "You once referred to your family that way."

She nodded, her expression watchful.

"This all sounds like some movie of the week."

"Yeah." Alex gave a short laugh. "Or a good book."

"Yet it all makes sense. Your eyes, the way you move, your confidence."

Brenna grinned. "Like that, do you?"

Alex coughed, drawing both their frowns. "Still, we are not human."

"Are you immortal?"

"No. Though we heal much faster, our life spans are the same as yours."

Tilting his head, Carson considered the woman he

loved. "Let me get this straight. You live, you die. You eat, you sleep, you breathe. Like me. Right?"

Brenna nodded, her expression tight.

"So the only difference is that you can change into a wolf at will."

Again she gave a nod, still watching Carson with shuttered eyes.

Throat tight, Carson managed to lift one shoulder in a shrug. "So who cares?" He took a deep, shuddering breath, trying to take it all in, knowing he couldn't, not yet. So instead he focused on what he did know, what really mattered. *Love.*

"I love you." He swallowed. "And I think you love me, too. I've been given a second chance. I don't want to waste it. What we have between us is special. I took it for granted once. I won't make that mistake again."

Brenna's expression didn't change. "What about children?"

Children. For a moment Carson's heart constricted as he thought of his lost daughter, Becky. Could he have another child, take such a giant leap of blind faith? Then he remembered the love he'd seen shining in Brenna's eyes and knew he could.

"What happens with children born of a union between a human and a shape-shifter? Is such a thing possible?" he asked.

Alex answered, one corner of his mouth lifting in a wry smile. "We call them Changelings. They can change, though they are not as strong. Still, among our people, they're welcomed and loved."

Love. "That's all that matters."

"Then I give you my blessing." Alex sounded formal—and pleased.

"Wait." Brenna pushed herself away from Carson to stand. "You two are talking like I'm not here."

Alex grinned. "Sorry."

Holding her shoulder, she focused on Carson. "We've been through a lot together. I don't think you've had enough time to think this through."

"Time?" Carson ran a hand through his hair. "I've spent the past eighteen months shunning life, living in the past. I'm not avoiding life anymore. I love you. I want to spend the rest of my days with you."

She didn't move. "I was engaged once. His name was Jeff. He loved me, too, or so he said. Yet when he found out what I was, what I could do, he ran from me in horror. He lost his life that night, Carson. Because he couldn't face what I am."

"I know what you are."

"I want you to think about it." She went to her brother and placed a light kiss on his cheek. "If he has any questions, answer them."

Then, turning, she faced Carson from several feet away. "This distance between us feels like a chasm."

His heart sank. "Only if you make it one."

"Three days." Sadness clouded her eyes. "Meet me in the woods in three days. If you don't show up, I'll understand."

With an effort Carson tamped down his impatience. Not an easy task when every heartbeat, every breath, sounded out the need to convince her. "I won't change my mind."

Her smile was a pitiful attempt. "We'll see." She walked away, still holding her shoulder.

Carson started after her. Alex stood, blocking his path. "Let her go. She's right. Think about things.

Then, if in three days you still want her, both of you will be certain.''

Shoving his hands in his pockets, Carson swallowed. "I don't understand.''

"It's not often we mate with humans. To expose her true nature to you, Brenna took a terrible risk.''

"Did her fiancé really die?''

"Head-on collision. Killed instantly.''

Carson grimaced. "I guess I can understand her need to be certain." He started to turn away.

"I need to ask a favor.''

Something in the other man's tone stopped Carson in his tracks. A hint of desperation, tinged with worry and fear.

"Once this is all done, there will be a trial," Alex said. "I'll have to testify. I don't want anything to happen to Brenna if...''

The rest of his sentence hovered in the air, unsaid.

Pain blossomed as Carson thought of Alex, of Brenna, meeting the same fate as his family. Then, to his amazement, the pain slowly receded. He didn't hesitate. "I will protect her with my life.''

"I thought you would say that." Alex nodded. "You really love her, don't you?''

"Yes." With an effort of will, Carson kept his voice even. "I'll give her the time she wants, then I'll tell her again myself.''

"Three days." A fierce grin broke out across Alex's face. "Sunday evening. Meet me in the woods near the cemetery around seven. I'll take you to her then.''

"That's late. Make it earlier.''

"She needs time.''

"You're sure she's fine?''

"Yes. Agreed?"

Though his first impulse was to argue, Carson knew what the other man asked was fair. Or would be, if he were a reasonable man. Unfortunately, he'd wasted too much time to be sensible.

"I'll be there," he said, and got up to go.

"They'll need to talk to you now." Alex jerked his thumb toward the cluster of Feds.

"Later." Ignoring what he knew he should do, Carson headed out to the road and his battered Tahoe. "I've got a pet to look after."

Still waiting in the Tahoe, Phelan barked, standing with his front paws on the door, nose pressed against the window. As soon as Carson opened the truck door, the excited puppy jumped all over him, panting and licking furiously. No matter how often Carson rebuffed him, Phelan never cared. Wiggling his entire small body to match his wagging tail, he leaped on Carson with all the fervor of any well-loved pet greeting a beloved human.

Beloved human. Gathering Phelan to him, the thought shamed Carson. Because letting anyone, even a puppy, get close had terrified him, he had devoted all his energy into pushing the pup away.

As Phelan rained wet doggy kisses all over him, he realized he had a lot to make up for. In more than one way, he would be starting over.

Immediately he took Phelan to the woods. Somehow, he meant to find Brenna.

"Three days my ass," he told the puppy. He had to see Brenna now, to touch her with his own hands and make certain she was okay.

And he wanted to convince her how much he loved her.

Phelan barked, wanting out of his arms. Gently placing the puppy on the ground, Carson had an idea.

"Phelan." He put playful urgency in his tone. The puppy cocked his head, listening.

"Where's Brenna? Find Brenna."

With a small bark, the puppy took off running.

She heard them coming long before they neared her hiding place. In her wolf form, every sense became amplified, especially the sharpness of her hearing. So she listened and waited, trying to puzzle out the whys and the hows.

Carson knew what she was. He hadn't waited, as she'd asked. What had he decided?

First came Phelan, crashing through the forest, a bounding bundle of eagerness and joy. Brenna couldn't help but smile as only a wolf could.

And behind him, Carson. Moving more slowly, cautiously, though with no less purpose.

Carson. Her smile faded. Heart began to pound. She'd asked for three days. Had he made up his mind to leave so quickly?

Wavering, she stood on shaky legs and moved soundlessly farther into the shadows, where he couldn't see her.

"Hiding, sis?" Alex's voice.

She turned, saw her brother standing in his human form and began the change herself. It took only seconds for her to go from wolf to woman and step back into her clothes: then she was able to wrap herself in Alex's comforting arms and place her head on his broad chest.

"Are you all right?"

"I've healed my shoulder wound," she said. "But my heart? I'm not certain I can heal that."

"There, there." He stroked her hair as he'd done so many times before when they were small. "Talk to him, Brenna. Everything will be all right."

She raised her face to look at her brother's implacable expression, finding, as always, comfort and strength in his rugged features, so like her own, yet so different. His gaze, full of sympathy, had the inexplicable result of making her want to cry. Even as she thought it, her eyes filled.

"I never cry," she said, lifting her chin and swiping at her eyes.

"You never did," Alex agreed. "Even when you were small."

A tear spilled onto her cheek. "I love him so much."

The barest of smiles touched Alex's firm mouth. "Then be yourself. You can't lose."

"Be myself?"

"Confident. Daring. Fearless. Don't lose your tenacity now."

"Easy for you to say," she mumbled. "One eye open, remember? Carson saw me change."

"Mama was talking about our enemies when she told us that, Bren. Keep one eye open for trouble. Trouble, not our mates."

Mates. Her breath caught at the word. Alex was her twin. He knew. "Do you think he is?"

"Could be." He lifted one shoulder. "Only you know for sure."

She registered a certain sadness in her brother's rugged features. "I heard you were married."

"Yeah." For a moment pain shone stark in his

face. ''I sent her away, made her disappear for her own safety. Once all this is over, I'll find her and settle things between us.''

He would, too, Brenna knew. Once Alex set his mind to something, he wouldn't rest until he'd accomplished his goal. She wished him happiness.

Phelan's tinny bark echoed through the woods, closer.

Alex smiled. ''It's only a matter of time before your pup finds us.''

''Change,'' she whispered urgently.

''Brenna…''

With one last desperate look at Alex, Brenna gave herself over to the change. In her wolf form, with her human emotions subjugated, she felt more capable of doing what she had to do.

Carson saw them first, two immense silver wolves standing in the shadows. When Phelan caught their scent, he hesitated in his stride, whining as he sat back on his haunches. He looked up at Carson as if asking for protection.

''It's all right, buddy,'' Carson said, awkwardly reaching down and scratching the puppy behind the ears. He eyed the magnificent animals. ''Just Brenna and Alex, waiting for us.''

The larger of the two wolves glided forward. Phelan scrambled to hide behind Carson's leg, trembling. The wolf stopped and cocked his head, tongue lolling. Carson could have sworn he was grinning.

Then Carson slid his gaze to the second wolf.

''Brenna.''

At her name she came forward, past the first wolf to halt a few feet from Carson. So close he recognized

Brenna's beloved brown eyes shining in the wolf's aristocratic face.

Then she changed.

Contrary to the old horror movies, there was nothing brutal or horrific about the transformation. One moment a regal silver wolf stood before him, the next, Brenna's slender form. The air had seemed to shimmer, her image wavered for an instant, then she was there. Naked, her beauty took his breath away. Then she stepped behind a tree, reappearing in a long, flowing dress.

When she changed to face Carson as a human, so, too, did Alex. Smiling, he dressed, then reached for the surprised Phelan, scooping him up in his arms and crooning wordlessly. He winked at Carson as they walked away.

"You've come to say goodbye," Brenna said, her expression solemn, pain evident in the careful way she enunciated each word.

"No." He shook his head. "You of all people should know—" Unable to continue, he swallowed. Hard. To try for a second chance at life, at love, was not a thing to be attempted lightly. What he would do if she refused him, he couldn't contemplate.

Brenna.

When he'd regained his composure, he took one step. Only one. Watching and hoping and praying— yes, praying—she would give him some sort of sign.

"What do you want?" Her features were as blank as her tone. "If it's absolution, I give it freely."

"Absolution?" Humbled, he looked away. Then, unable to help himself, he dragged his gaze back to her face.

"For doubting my brother," she said. What she meant, he knew, was "for doubting me."

She shrugged, a careless gesture, but he wasn't fooled. He saw how much she cared in the rigid way she held her slender body, poised as though on the edge of flight.

Or of changing.

He stepped forward again, not stopping until he stood mere inches from her. She lifted her chin, false bravado evidenced by the sheen in her eyes.

"I never doubted you," he said. Then, wanting to be totally honest, he added, "Maybe in the beginning, a little. But not after that."

She opened her mouth and closed it.

He moved toward her until his breath mingled with hers. Then he kissed her. Her nose. Her forehead. Her cheeks. And finally her lips.

"I love you." He whispered the words inside her mouth, knowing she heard them from the way she went utterly, totally still. So he lifted his lips from hers and said them again. "I love you. All of you."

This time it was she who reached up and pulled his face down to hers. As she kissed him, he tasted the salt of her tears and knew himself to be the luckiest man in the world.

Still, he had to make certain she understood.

"I can't do anything as exotic as change into a wolf," he said, smiling. "But I will cherish you and love you with all of my heart."

Her eyes were bright with tears and fierce with emotion. With love.

"Wolves mate for life," she warned him.

He laughed. "I wouldn't have it any other way."

* * * * *

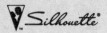
INTIMATE MOMENTS™

A new generation searches for truth...
From award-winning author

Marie Ferrarella

Immovable Objects

(Silhouette Intimate Moments #1305)

Feisty and beautiful Elizabeth Caldwell has finally
struck out on her own and is deep into her first
solo mission to help billionaire Cole Williams
recover a priceless piece of stolen art. Although
she'd vowed never to get caught up with another
controlling man, Cole's devastating good looks—
coupled with the thrill of the hunt—sweep her
right off her feet. But she has to stay in control and
in the game, for it's her mysterious powers alone
that can save them from the grave danger that
threatens to consume them both.

FAMILY
SECRETS
THE NEXT GENERATION

Available July 2004 at your favorite retail outlet.

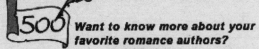

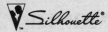

Silhouette®

COMING NEXT MONTH